CSF

P9-CBB-486

A WYATT BOOK for
ST. MARTIN'S PRESS

Beverly & Marigold

Val Coleman

Illustrations by Bill Woodman

a Wyatt Book for St. Martin's Press

New York

BEVERLY & MARIGOLD. Copyright © 1996 by Val Coleman. All rights reserved. Printed in the United States of America. No part of this book may be used or reproduced in any manner whatsoever without written permission except in the case of brief quotations embodied in critical articles or reviews. For information, address A Wyatt Book for St. Martin's Press, 175 Fifth Avenue, New York, N.Y. 10010.

Illustrations by Bill Woodman. Copyright © 1996.

Design by Songhee Kim

Library of Congress Cataloging-in-Publication Data

Coleman, Val.
    Beverly & Marigold   /   Val Coleman.—1st ed.
      p. cm.
    "A Wyatt book for St. Martin's Press."
    ISBN 0-312-14549-7 (hardcover)
    1. United States—Social life and customs—20th century—
Fiction. 2. New York (N.Y.)—Social life and customs—Fiction.
3. Afro—American politicians—New York (N.Y.)—Fiction.
4. Homeless women—New York (N.Y.)—Fiction. I. Title.
PS3553.O47446B48 1996   96-3096 .
813'.54—dc20   CIP

First Edition: November 1996

10 9 8 7 6 5 4 3 2 1

To Charlie, of course.

Author's Note

Although I am Beverly and the Beverly stories are full of things that happened, I have turned things upside down and added this and added that and the result is pure fiction.

Val Coleman

Contents

Preface

EVERYONE LIES. IT's part of the truth. For example, I've taken to running around recently and telling everyone what a swell fella I am, practically a Prince of Peace who, like a crazy postman, will deliver Thanksgiving turkeys all year round in all kinds of weather. I even wrote this book, the one you're reading right now, to set my better angels up in front where you can see them clearly and applaud.

That's one part of the truth. The other part can be found in the bloodstream of this book, and that's a lot harder to explain.

The book really has a bloodstream, a river inside that keeps it alive. It begins in the heart of the country, in Illinois, where the great American rivers meet, stops off for a lot of drinks in Ohio where I get a raggedy education and ends up on the streets of New York City where Beverly meets Marigold and the prose changes from the cranky inconstance of the truth to a series of songs about the underbelly of a city that I have grown to love.

In a way, that explains everything and I should stop the preface right here. But I can't stop because I have to tell you about the onion man.

You see, this is a crazy river of a book that runs up-and downhill and must be understood as the handiwork of an American eccentric, an onion man.

Let me explain. There was a period in the seventies when I was in and out of Alcoholics Anonymous like a carpenter's elbow. During those little patches of sobriety I would grandstand by racing around the city in my company car picking up drunks and delivering them to the Swedish Hospital in Brooklyn, which had a ghastly flight deck where alcoholics would go through a terrible, lonely withdrawal.

One day I found an enormous khaki-colored ball, about four feet in diameter with a head and two feet on either end, lying on the sidewalk outside Sammy's Bowery Follies. I rolled it into the back of the car and headed for Brooklyn. On the other side of the Brooklyn Bridge I stopped for a minute and gave him a long pull on a pint bottle of Scotch that I kept in the glove compartment to prevent convulsions. When we got to Swedish Hospital, I started to peel off the blankets. He was an onion. Peel after peel came off and the ball got smaller and smaller until this bright white nude man lay there exposed and defenseless, as if we had gone back in time to the earliest child of mankind in the most ancient savannah and suddenly he became the most precious thing on earth. Worth saving. Oh God worth saving.

Each of us is an onion man, putting on and taking off our blankets, each swaddled in absurdity.

But everyone is worth the candle.

I think that's what this book's about.

Beverly
&
Marigold

The Stamp Collection

So there I was in Charleston, Illinois, ten years old on a summer morning in 1941, the year the war began for us, making a life out of BB guns, crabapple trees, and Burton Barnes's Ping-Pong table.

On that morning my mother had a memorable visit from Shirley Trimble. Shirley Trimble was a guy with a girl's name. Since I had been named Beverly, I had a special admiration for Shirley Trimble. I liked to think I knew what he had been through as a kid, although the real truth was that nobody ever bothered me once I learned to yell "Yes!" whenever anybody asked me if my name was Beverly. Shirley was a good friend of my mother's, and since he was a fallen-away Catholic, she was always trying to get him to go to Mass. He humored her by listening carefully when she slapped up a sermon in our kitchen when he came to visit.

More important than anything else, Shirley Trimble was an antique dealer and my mother was a nut for antiques. His visits were always announced by wonderful noises— great *clanks* and *dongs* as he would wrestle whatever he was trying to sell Mom out of his old panel truck and onto our little front porch. That morning it was a big old wooden box with spindly legs.

"Shirley!" my mom sang out, "what do you expect me to do with another credenza?"

"Credenza?!" Shirley sounded shocked. "Where do you see a credenza? This is an honest-to-God old-fashioned, mint-condition, metal-faced pie pantry! Probably the only one left in America!"

"Pie pantry?" Mom's voice softened. "You have a pie pantry?"

"There she is," said Shirley, and he turned it dramatically so that Mom could see the gray metal with holes in it that filled up the paned doors on the fancy front.

"A real, old pie pantry." Mom was gone.

"Seventy-five dollars," said Shirley.

Mom was gone but not crazy. "Twenty dollars, next payday."

"Fifty."

"Thirty-five, Shirley. We're poor people, and Sam's goin' to shoot me when he gets home from school."

"Deal," said Shirley.

My dad, Samuel Taylor Reynolds, was a fine professor of history at Eastern Illinois State Teachers College. He wouldn't shoot anybody, least of all my mother, who he loved so much he would call the hospital when she got a cold.

You could just see how pleased Mom was with her pie pantry; she right away got out her soft dustcloths and was dusting the tops of the doors and spit cleaning the metal inserts before it was even in the house.

That morning, Shirley had a private talk with my mother. The odd thing was that despite the fact I hadn't

3

done anything wrong that I could remember, certainly nothing involving Shirley, I knew the talk they were having was about me.

You know how kids are, with secrets and things. They may sleep without dreaming, but they sure as hell worry in the daytime.

Anyway, the two of them sat down in the front room and talked for a good ten minutes. I could see them through the big corner window next to the porch, and it looked like a regular conversation. Mom didn't faint, flinch or raise her hand to her mouth, so I figured it wasn't the biggest deal in the world.

Mom eventually came to the door and asked me to come in and I did and I sat next to her on the big green couch.

"Mr. Trimble wants you to do something for him, Beverly, and I think it's a good idea."

"Bev," said Shirley Trimble, "my wife, Olga, is sickly. Nothin' catchin'," he added quickly, "but she needs looking after when I'm away at the shop or making deliveries. Since this is summer and you're out of school, I thought maybe you could give me a hand."

"Well I guess so, Mr. Trimble," I said, having the first adult conversation of my life.

"I wouldn't ask you to do it for nothing, Beverly." And Shirley Trimble reached down next to him in the chair and pulled up a large flat package wrapped in brown paper and tied up with red string. "If you do a good job and watch over her, I'll give you what's in this package."

"What's that, Mr. Trimble?"

He started untying and unfolding right away until a great orange book appeared. When he set aside the brown paper, the paper stayed the same shape it was when it was wrapped, so that book must have been wrapped up that way a long long time ago.

"It's an American stamp collection and it's the best I ever saw."

Now I didn't know much about stamp collections, but I have to tell you how I felt the first time I saw that orange book open on the round coffee table in our front room. I can still see the wonderful colored pictures of mysterious places like Chicago and the western desert. I can see the snowy landscape of Wisconsin and the upper tier. I can see New England cottages and New Orleans black dancers and the cameo profiles of a dozen men from George Washington to Jefferson Davis.

Maybe I've added a few pictures over the years that really weren't there at the time, but I know for sure that when I unlocked my ten-year-old eyes that morning I found things much more wonderful than the saints in the stained-glass windows at St. Charles Borromeo Catholic Church or even Burton Barnes's Ping-Pong table.

Mr. Trimble was a kind man, but those were hard days and he was not going to give me the stamp collection until I had earned it and he gently pulled it over to his side of the coffee table and rewrapped it, asking me to put my finger on the string so he could tie off the knot again.

He said, "Come over to my house tomorrow morning

at eleven and we'll get started." As he left, I couldn't take my eyes off the package under his arm. He winked a grand wink at me—he knew exactly what a ruckus he had caused in our house that summer morning. My mother and I had both fallen in love, she with the pie pantry and me with the rest of the world.

WELL, YOU KNOW where I was at eleven o'clock sharp the next morning. Much to my surprise, Mrs. Olga Trimble answered the doorbell herself at their house on Tenth Street and stood there looking, as far as I could tell, very healthy. I had met her a couple of times before and she was always kind to me, although she was fat enough to scare me a little when I got very close to her. I heard Shirley's voice in the background, "Come on in, Bev, and take a load off." He stood beside his wife as I opened the milk-glass front door and stepped into the living room.

"No reason, Shirley," said Mrs. Trimble, "for the boy to come today. I'm feeling fit, and Mrs. Quimby is coming over to read for an hour this afternoon."

"Well," said Shirley, "I thought he ought to get the lay of the land, and that old bat Quimby's gonna run out of things to read one of these days."

I had no idea what they were talking about, but the truth is all three of us smiled when Shirley called this Mrs. Quimby an "old bat."

"There are twenty-six sermons," Mrs. Trimble replied with her hand over her mouth so I couldn't see the smile, "and she's hardly read three up till now, so there's plenty yet to go."

Shirley had his hat on. "You stay around till Mrs. Quimby comes," he instructed me, "and Olga will show you the place where she likes to rest and how to make the bandages."

But he turned in the doorway and a strange look came over his face. It was a pleading, honest look, and his voice came out thin and different when he spoke. "Olga," he began so quietly that I could barely hear him, "I heard of a man up in Kankakee yesterday who's got some new ideas about this thing and . . ."

"You mean a *doctor* up in Kankakee, don't you, Shirley Trimble?"

"Well now, I ain't sure," Shirley said right away as if he knew what she was going to ask before she asked it. "I'm not sure at all. He's got some kind of place up there, and they got some government money to study blood." Shirley seemed pleased that she was listening so he went ahead fast. "You see, darlin', we're gonna be in this war sure as hell, and the government figures we better know as much as we can about blood, there's gonna be a lot of it spilt before we're through. So I figured, you and I could take a run up there this Saturday and talk to this man. . . ."

"I've been wondering . . ." started Olga. Shirley turned around abruptly, took off his hat, and came all the way back into the living room. It looked like he was amazed that she was not dismissing his idea. He was all ears.

"I've been wondering if I may be some kind of

7

bleeding person that God set down on this earth just at this time, to let us know how terrible these wars are and make us mind our manners."

Shirley sat down sadly, defeated once again. "Oh God, no, Olga. You are plain sick, like the kings of Europe, and it's got no plan at all, just plain bad luck. I thought maybe this man in Kankakee . . ."

Olga put her arms around her husband, who was now sitting in the rocking chair. "I know how much you want to help, old Shirley, but you know there can't be any doctors. We'll find it, don't you worry, we'll find the truth and it will heal me up."

Shirley suddenly remembered that I was standing there, listening to all of this, and he found a smile.

"Look here, Beverly." Shirley was on his feet, and he walked to an old sideboard table in the dining room where, believe it or not, the big orange book lay unwrapped. "I thought I'd leave this out for you and Olga to study. She knows all about these stamps and the places that they come from. By the time she's well again, you'll be a regular expert on the United States of America."

He looked back at his wife with that pleading look of his and walked on out the door.

That first day was a wonderful day. Mrs. Trimble took me on the first leg of a grand journey. She pulled up the leaf of that sideboard table and it snapped into place. That gave us plenty of room to open the orange book. I pulled over two chairs with wicker seats, and she opened the book to a page with six stamps from Niagara Falls. Some were red and some were blue, but they all had that great flood of water tumbling down the side of a mountain and, if you looked very closely, you could see the tiny boat that Olga said was called the *Maid of the Mist* down where a cloud of water fog rose at the bottom of the falls.

"We were on that boat," Olga said, leaning back in her chair as she talked with her eyes passing right over my head. "Shirley and me couldn't say nothing to each other because of the roar of the water, but we were happy. He had a big old oil slicker of a raincoat that he wrapped around both of us, and we just held on. It was like standing in the middle of a symphony orchestra, right next to the double basses." And she went right over to the record player, turned it on, unsheathed an old 78 shellac record, popped it over the center spindle, and put on the cactus needle.

She told me it was Beethoven, and the room roared with the basses and the cellos playing the same music at the same time and she came over and stood next to me like we were on the *Maid of the Mist,* riding the bumpy seas beneath the falls. I was only ten, and her hand rested lightly on my shoulder, but I could really tell how important this great noisy memory was to her. I wasn't even scared of her being fat anymore. In fact I even reached up and gave her hand a squeeze, a grown-up thing for me to do and she looked down at me for the first time and was very grateful.

It was the first time, by the way, that I had paid any attention to classical music. I hadn't made any connection between those complicated chords that my mother and my sister kept in the music room at our house and the things I felt. The music was stored in big green albums and I couldn't stand any of them except one little album with Fats Waller on it singing "Your Feet's Too Big."

But Mrs. Trimble's Beethoven was different. I actually heard all of the different instruments, and they made me feel the thunder and the power of Niagara Falls.

I guess the doorbell started ringing before the Beethoven record was finished, but we didn't know anybody was at the door until Mrs. Quimby started banging so hard we couldn't miss it. Mrs. Trimble went over to the record player, lifted the needle, stopped the music, and then did a curious thing. She put her finger to her mouth and shushed me.

Now Mrs. Quimby wasn't so bad after all, although Mrs. Trimble and I exchanged secret smiles when she came in. I think Mrs. Trimble actually waved her arms like an "old bat" just before Mrs. Quimby came through the front door. Anyway, she had me laughing enough so Mrs. Quimby looked at me peculiar when she first caught sight of me.

The thing that I remember about how Mrs. Quimby looked was that she was tall and skinny and old, like the elm outside my sister's window in the wintertime. From her topmost branches, she looked down at me and said, "Olga, who's this?"

"This is my friend Beverly Reynolds," Olga said protectively, and I was grateful because I figured I needed a friend with this old elm tree about to fall on me.

Mrs. Quimby surprised me with a smile of her own, and then she said a most peculiar thing, " 'Damsel, I say unto thee, arise!' "

"Mrs. Quimby is speaking scripture, Beverly."

"It's what Jesus said when he cured the ruler's daughter," explained Mrs. Quimby, who added, "I'm pleased to meet you, Beverly."

My mother had taught me to take no guff from anyone, so I said, real quietly, "I'm not a damsel."

"Speak up!" instructed Mrs. Quimby.

"I ain't no damsel!" I said real loud like Beethoven would have said it, and Mrs. Quimby put down the yellow book she was holding in her hand and took hold of my shoulder.

"My apologies, Mr. Beverly Reynolds. I can see right now that Sister Olga has a good and brave friend."

Well, this was a day for strong new words. It felt especially good to be called brave, and I decided that people called Mrs. Quimby an old bat because of the way she looked and not the way she was.

As I left the house that morning, I remember looking back at the milk-glass front door, open just a few inches, and the small white face of Olga Trimble smiling at me, the way you smile at someone when you've made a good new friend.

I know I said that kids don't dream, but that night I dreamed dreams of falling water and loud bass fiddles. I also dreamed about Mrs. Trimble's mouth, and just inside her lips I could see a circle of caked brown blood.

✷ ✷ ✷

TWO MORNINGS LATER, Shirley Trimble called and asked me if I'd come down to his house right away. He said that Mrs. Trimble had "taken a turn."

I ran most of the way down Tenth Street to their house with another brand-new feeling, this one in my stomach. It felt the same as being very hungry, only I'd just had hot oatmeal and two big vitamin pills.

Shirley was gone when I got to the Trimbles' house, so Mrs. Quimby opened the door and let me in. She had that little yellow book in her hand, and just as soon as she had said hello, she had her nose back in the book and was reading out loud about the "Science of the Mortal Mind" and other such stuff. She didn't stop reading out loud even while she was in the middle of sitting down, and for the first time that morning, I saw poor Mrs. Trimble.

Olga Trimble was asleep on a special bed in the living room, and she was wrapped in what looked like a bunch of white sheets. They were tucked all around her and tied off in different places. I knew she was alive because I could hear the bellows of her breathing underneath the rhythms of Mrs. Quimby's voice as she read from the yellow book.

We just sat there, Mrs. Quimby and I, for a long long time. Her voice had a steady tempo, and it must have been almost an hour later when Mrs. Quimby stopped reading, closed her book quietly, put on her hat with a long stickpin, and said good-bye.

Mrs. Trimble and I were alone, and I was scared.

12

I didn't see it right away because I had been staring so hard at Mrs. Trimble's sleeping face.

All at once my eyes focused, and I suddenly could see this long red stain appearing sharply against the white sheet near the middle of Mrs. Trimble's body. Mrs. Trimble woke up at that very moment and immediately saw the frightened look on my face. She looked down at the stain and instinctively brought her hand down to cover it, but the stain had grown larger than her hand.

"Never mind, Bev," she said to me. "Get one of those sheets over on the side table and bring it here." Her voice was surprisingly strong, and she added, "While you're at it, bring the stamp collection to me."

Mrs. Trimble was a remarkable woman. Waking up from a sound sleep, she instantly cared more about my feelings than her own belly, which apparently was bleeding pretty badly. I got the sheet and picked up the stamp collection that was also on the side table and brought them both over to her. Winding the sheet around and under her by rolling back and forth, she covered up the stain in a couple of minutes as I stood helplessly by, not knowing what to do. When she was finished and no more red stain could be seen, she breathed a long sigh and adjusted the pillow behind her head.

"Now, Bev," she said a little breathlessly, "let's see what stamp we've got today."

Now let me remind you that I was ten years old in the summer of 1941, and I was very confused by all these things that were going on in Shirley and Olga Trimble's living room. I didn't know what I was supposed to do, so I said, "Mrs. Trimble, do you want me to call up Shirley or a doctor or somebody? Seems like I ought to do something to help you with all that bleeding and there's nobody here but me and you and . . ."

"God's here too, Bev, don't you worry. He and I've been through this before, and I came out just fine. Hand me that stamp book."

So I handed it over without another word. There was something in her voice that sounded so sure that I figured it was the only thing to do.

"Here we are!" Mrs. Trimble was excited. "I found it on the first page I turned to!" She was pointing to a black and white stamp that was printed in the middle of the page. It wasn't the real stamp at all, just a picture of it where you were supposed to paste the real stamp when you got it. It was a picture of an American soldier with a big tin hat. He had funny looking pants that were like my old knickers, and he was holding a big long gun out in front of him with a bayonet on the end. It was a three-cent stamp, and I could see in the background the flags of different countries, including the USA.

"A commemorative stamp of the Great War, Bev, just ended twenty-three years ago," she said, and her eyes looked above my head again.

"That was my Shirley, that boy there on the stamp, and how handsome he was!"

Then, without warning, she sat up in bed and grasped my hand in both of hers. "Oh my God, Beverly, it's going to happen again!" Her eyes were dimmed with tears. "Don't believe them! Don't let them have you . . . not this time!"

All I could think of to say was, "Don't worry, Mrs. Trimble, I'll be okay."

But she was frantic. "No. You must run and hide from them. You must!" She looked upward again, and her voice sounded as if she were singing, a thin, keening soprano.

"By the time Shirley got to France, they had forgotten why they were fighting. They had forgotten why they were angry at each other. At Christmastime the soldiers stood up in the trenches and held tiny Christmas trees above their heads, and for a time, the killing stopped. They had forgotten why they went to war."

She was sobbing. "I remember a poem," she went on. "There were so many poems, I don't know who wrote it.

> *We are the dead. Short days ago*
> *We lived, felt dawn, saw sunset glow . . .*

"Shirley was a medic and so he saw the worst of it. Everyone was maimed or died. Shirley lost half of his lung in a gas attack. Both sides!" She squeezed my hand so hard it hurt. "Both sides filled the air with poison gas."

She stopped for a moment and then ended her refrain.

"I was very beautiful, you know. Those old men in their old dusty governments, they took away my time. . . ."

She closed the book, looked at me gratefully, and fell asleep again.

When I got home that night, I wanted to talk to my father about Mrs. Trimble and the war and lots of other

15

things. It was an important evening in my life, and the ordinary things like supper and the argument about my sister's pigtail seemed stupid since my head was rocking with brand-new ideas and awakenings that came in bits and pieces. Both of my parents were much too busy to talk to me that evening, so I went to my room, sat down, and for some reason that I can't explain, began to cry.

I think it is a special time in life, the first time you cry for someone other than yourself.

Over the summer and on into the fall, I must have visited Mrs. Trimble a dozen times. When she wasn't asleep we studied the stamps, and she explained the secrets of the mole on Abraham Lincoln's face and the Great Smoky Mountains, and I was always sad when Mrs. Quimby came to relieve me and send me home.

One fall day when the leaves were as beautiful as the painting on Mrs. Trimble's parlor wall, I went on over to her house and peeked through the clear glass edge of the milk-glass door before I rang the bell. I was happy to see Mrs. Trimble sitting up in a big upholstered chair with her regular clothes on, and when I came in she gave me a big smile and a kiss although she didn't stand up.

Mrs. Quimby was already there and reading in her regular chair. She put down her yellow book long enough to speak to me.

"Beverly," said Mrs. Quimby, "do you believe in God?"

"Sure, Mrs. Quimby."

"And Jesus Christ, his son, who came to earth to heal us?"

"Sure, Mrs. Quimby."

"That's a good boy, Beverly. I know your mother is a Roman, but you'll be fine when you grow up and think about these days when Christ the Scientist made Mrs. Trimble well."

"Sure, Mrs. Quimby," I said, wishing I knew what she was talking about. I sat there quietly as Mrs. Quimby finished the sermon she was reading, secretly hoping that she'd disappear so that Mrs. Trimble and I could get down to the serious business of the stamps.

Mrs. Quimby finally stopped, put the stickpin in her hat, and closed the door behind her.

In a second, Olga Trimble was rubbing her hands together in glee. "Go get it, Bev," she instructed and I ran to the sideboard and picked up the stamp collection. Full of anticipation, I handed it to her and I had the good sense to say, "You look much better, Mrs. Trimble."

She said, "Much better, Beverly," and smiled a big smile as she riffled through the pages of the stamp collection.

"You pick a stamp," she said, and I stuck my finger in the flying pages and the book fell open on Mrs. Trimble's lap.

And there it was, near the top of the page, a big rectangular red stamp, a picture of a steam locomotive coming right at me with a big white round headlight and a whole string of cars behind it curving up from the back. You could see the smokestack and a beautiful splash of white smoke across the top of the stamp.

"Oh, my," said Mrs. Trimble, "anybody with any sense gotta love those steam engines." And she seemed so satisfied that she sat in silence for a full minute or two until she looked, as she always looked, above my head.

"Right after the war we went up to Chicago, thundered up there on the Illinois Central," it was that singing voice of hers again, "and I thought that the big city was cockeyed beautiful with all the boxcars and the tall buildings and the stockyards on the lake. I thought it was good to be alive when we took the Great Northern west along through Wisconsin and Minnesota, it was winter you know, and the night passages with tiny lights cast across the snow were something Shirley and me will never forget. We went all the way west that winter, all the way to California. We saw buffalo, we really saw buffalo, there were still buffalo on the western plain after the war. And the Pacific Ocean, the ocean of peace, was so beautiful I had to squint so I could take it in a little bit at a time.

"We were lookin' all over for a doctor who could stop my bleeding. Shirley was bound and determined to find what all the royal families of Europe couldn't find, a way to stop my bleeding. You see, I have something that has a lovely name, the Christmas disease, a kind of hemophilia that only women can get so nobody's paid much attention."

"Did you find a doctor?" I asked, hoping it was the right thing to ask because I didn't understand much of anything she'd said. But I did understand that she wanted to talk about it, even if it was just talking to a ten-year-old kid.

"I guess we did find a doctor, if you think about it. Shirley heard about some fella in Chicago and we went to see him and he just took our money. There was a much nicer man in Minnesota, who plain admitted there was nothing he could do, and by the time we got to San Francisco, we'd spent Shirley's army mustering-out pay and the doctor there didn't charge us because he couldn't do anything either.

"We came back on the Santa Fe and stopped for a while in the New Mexican desert where we met this old woman of God who said she believed in Christ the Scientist, and she told us that the only way to heal the sick was to find the truth. I felt that was the most honest thing I'd heard so far and got better right away."

Mrs. Trimble leaned way down and whispered in my ear. She was so close that I could see that her eyes were shot with blood and her breath smelled like wet ashes. "I'll tell you a secret, Beverly," she whispered. "I'm not sure I'm getting better. Seems to me there's much more to this than meets the eye. When Shirley was in France I bled something terrible. I was bruised all over when they were killing one another. Then, after the war ended, we took this trip and I got well somehow. Now, with the shooting and the killing back again, I have terrible spells and bruises and I'm not real sure that even Mrs. Quimby can help me."

Just as she said that Shirley Trimble opened the front door and with a big smile on his face said, "What have you two been up to?" And he leaned down and kissed his wife very tenderly on her forehead. "So good to see you out of that bed, old Olga. Seems like the boy is the best physician of them all!"

Mrs. Trimble smiled a big wide smile. She took both our hands, and the three of us stood there for a moment like a family picture.

That night I got in real trouble. I knocked on the door of my father's study and he told me to come in. "I'm awful busy, Bev," he said, pointing to a pile of blue folders on his desk, "but what's the problem?"

"It's about Mrs. Trimble."

Dad glanced up, "You've been sitting with her, haven't you? Any troubles?"

"What's Christmas disease, Dad?"

He shook his head and smiled, "Damned if I know. Too many presents, maybe?"

I said, "It's also called hemo . . . hemophilia or something, and poor Mrs. Trimble's got it awful bad."

"How do you know that?" I had my father's full attention.

"Well, once I saw her bleeding and there was nothing I could do."

"Oh my God," said my father. "Dorothee!" he called out loud and went into the kitchen and closed the door.

I guess I'd set off some big storm at my house. My folks decided that I wasn't to sit with Mrs. Trimble anymore. I was forbidden to go to her house, and Mom called up Shirley Trimble to explain. Although I was angry at the time, when I was older I understood what they had done. How could they possibly know the magical things that Mrs.

Trimble and I had shared? How could they know that I was a brand-new, different person?

Four more weeks went by, and some days I would even forget about Mrs. Trimble and the stamp collection. And then came the first Sunday in December of 1941. Everyone who was alive that day remembers where he was when the news came. I was in the front seat of our old Ford near the railroad tracks on the way to the Whelans' farm when the announcer on the car radio said the Japanese had bombed Pearl Harbor.

I don't know why exactly, but I asked my dad to stop the car, and I got out and started running toward Mrs. Trimble's house. As I ran along the streets, everyone's door was opening and the voice of that radio announcer was everywhere. All the radios were on and became one giant radio voice that filled the air. By the time I got to Tenth Street I was pretty tired. Way on down the block I could see a red light blinking on top of an ambulance in front of Mrs. Trimble's house. Shirley Trimble was on his lawn, talking to some men when he saw me coming as fast as I could run.

His eyes were full of tears and he said, "Oh Beverly, she asked for you all morning and I couldn't find you. I didn't know what to do."

The door of the Trimble house opened, and two men carried my friend Olga Trimble on a stretcher to the ambulance. She was covered completely with one of the white sheets. I could just see a little bit of her hair falling beyond the end of the stretcher.

The voice of the announcer was saying, "Hundreds, maybe thousands may have died this morning trapped in the holds of the battleships. . . ."

Just before the ambulance pulled away, Shirley Trimble leaned down to me and said, "She's dead, old Bev, and I don't know what I'll do."

He looked up at me once more. He could barely speak, "There's something for you on the side table." And he pointed at the door as the ambulance hurried him away.

I walked up the stairs and opened the milk-glass door and went into the living room. All I could see was the orange book, sitting there on the side table as it always had. I picked it up carefully and saw that someone had marked a place with a piece of paper.

I carried the book out on the front porch and sat in the porch swing where I had never sat before. I carefully opened the book to the page with the slip of paper, and there, spread out across two pages, were at least a hundred big old stamps, all different colors, each one the picture of an airplane.

And on the slip of paper, a note had been carefully written:

Dear Beverly,

I'm sorry I can't see you anymore. These are airmail stamps, the first airmail stamps ever printed. I want you to promise me that you'll take care of them, take care of all the stamps in the book. Shirley and me never took an airplane ride, but I suppose you'll take a lot of them. I know I said some sad things when

we were together and I hope you weren't upset. I never had a
child, you know, and I must have borrowed you awhile.

Have a happy life, Beverly, and write me a letter someday.
Maybe you can mail it with one of these beautiful stamps.

Your good friend,
Olga Trimble

This is that letter.

The Gentle Man

My Second World War was filled with improbable heroes, not the usual run of brave machine gunners but a bunch of odd ducks that were bit players during the great killing time.

I was ten to fifteen years old during the war, right on the cusp of puberty, and my main hero was my high school coach, a man named P. J. Van Horn, a gentle man who paid attention to me and tendered me through a time when everybody else, including my parents, was much too busy prosecuting Adolf Hitler to manage a backsliding adolescent.

We know a good deal about unattended young boys nowadays, how they often turn into predators on the streets of big cities, so in order to tell the story of my rescue by P. J. Van Horn during the years of the "good" war, I must begin by telling the story of my family's trek across the country in 1943 from small town Charleston, Illinois, to the engine of World War II, Washington, D.C.

My father was a teacher and a patriot who had soldiered in the First World War and almost died in France in that terrible flu epidemic but survived to become a history teacher in Charleston, Illinois. Charleston was Abraham Lincoln country, and my dad became a Lincoln scholar with a fierce loyalty to the nation that Lincoln had so patiently healed.

So when the new war came along with its certified villains, Dad found out that he was too old to join the army, so he packed up the whole family, including my mother and sister (my brother Charles had joined the marines and was God knows where), and took us to Washington, D.C., where he had finagled a job with the Office of War Information. My willful and wonderful mother wanted a piece of Hitler too, and she got a job in Washington with the Post Office Department, leaving me to my own devices in a city that had to ignore its youngest children in order to serve its children-soldiers.

I quickly became a most unpleasant young man.

It was a savage time in America, and the tempo of the streets of Washington reflected the hurtful mission of the war. Even my Catholic confirmation as a "soldier of Christ" during a two-day retreat in the crypt at Washington Cathedral was a violent affair complete with an enormous priest dressed in black and with ardent eyes, who scared the living hell out of me and a roomful of other thirteen-year-old boys with the infamous "hell sermon." It was a shouting, finger-pointing peroration that threatened us with eternal torture if we took our new impulses out of our underwear.

The sermon was followed by a harrowing run though the "catacombs," tunnels with the graves of monks and saints recessed in the walls, into a chamber full of confessional booths where I fell to my knees and admitted that I had peeked under my cousin Lucy's pinafore.

It seemed to me that all of this clerical savagery was part of the war effort.

Another savage, another of the odd "heroes" of my

war, was a fella named Big Hugo. Big Hugo shaved. He was also tall and was the leader and chief gangster of Taft Junior High School. Since I was a physical weakling and something of a coward, I became Big Hugo's "consigliore," his adviser and speechwriter, and, in return for his good opinion, I sat at his feet and nodded when he said wise things.

The worst thing I did that year in Washington was mistreat the one kid at school who was physically weaker than I. I have long since forgotten his name, but I remember his welcoming smile when we met. He immediately sensed that we were both frightened, and he reached out for my friendship with a touching intensity. He was scared just as I was scared in that big city school in the middle of a war. I answered his smile by putting my arm around his neck, and with his head locked against my side I dragged him up a long hill. He was helpless as I pulled my trophy past Big Hugo and his pals. At the top of the hill, I let him go and he ran away from me as fast as he could run because I had dishonored the secret understanding that the weaker people have with one another.

It was probably Big Hugo's plan to rob a bowling alley that woke me up. Until then I had been a very small-time criminal. I was stealing candy from the counter of the local drugstore, choosing Life Savers because they were round and easy to grab from the front of the display. And I put pennies on the streetcar tracks so that when streetcars ran over them, they flattened out to the size that fit in any coin machine that took a nickel.

One afternoon at school Big Hugo called the bowling alley meeting. He had it all figured out. Two guys would be lookouts, two guys with handkerchiefs on their faces like Jesse James would do the stickup, and we would all meet in the parking lot behind the Giant supermarket to split up the money.

The whole robbery was, of course, absurd. We didn't even have a gun and it was unlikely that the owner of the bowling alley was going to hand his money over to a couple of raggedy kids.

It was that night, the night after the meeting, that I suddenly understood that I was falling deeper and deeper into some dark hole that would swallow me up. And it was that night that I went to my mother and begged her to send me home to Illinois.

My mother, bless her, understood, and she immediately began to make arrangements for me to go back to Charleston and live with my only Charleston friend, Christopher Russell and his parents. I was to stay with them until the war ended and my family came home as well.

So, in April of 1945 I was put on a train and sent home with a suitcase full of chocolate bars. (My mother always hid candy in among my shirts because I loved candy and my mom loved me.)

I traveled to Illinois two days after President Roosevelt died, and the faces of my fellow passengers were gray, the kind of gray that isn't a color but a cast of sorrow that comes from deep inside us. I don't remember any words being spoken in my railroad car during that trip.

At the station in Mattoon, Illinois, Mrs. Russell met me and gave me a big kiss on the forehead, embarrassing the hell out of me. After all, now I was a big-shot city kid in a small-town puddle.

It didn't take me long to alienate everybody in town—kids, teachers, townspeople. Everybody but Chris and his mother. Chris, a sensitive young man with a badly deformed back, sort of cut a path for me through the schoolyard, making sure I wasn't left alone. I did my best to destroy that friendship too, but I never succeeded. Years later, I understood how lucky I had been in 1945 to have a friend like Chris who had done the best he could to guide me through that bumpy time in my life.

And that brings me to the gentle man. Chris, after all, was only fourteen and couldn't be expected to clean up the act of a newly minted pain in the ass like me. The man who did that was Coach Van Horn.

He shambled. P. J. Van Horn was a big, fleshy man who loved to eat chocolate doughnuts, providing a terrible example for his students. He was, after all, the high school football and basketball coach, and we almost never won a game. Coach Van Horn wasn't exactly fat, but he walked like a fat man and his clothes were draped on him like a fat man. But he was smart and wise, smart enough to be the general science teacher as well as coach and wise enough to get my number right away.

Coach Van Horn was also an exasperating man. He cut against the grain of the whole country. He was a man of peace in a time of war. He was a football coach who hated violence. He was a basketball coach who taught us to shoot free throws underhand.

And he was a gentle, compassionate teacher who cared much more about his students than about winning. He actually believed that high school sports were about growing up, not smashing mouths and victories at any cost. He had a terrible case of chronic bronchitis, a wheezing, spitting spasm of a disease that would attack him in the middle of his most important sentences.

He also had the town's most beautiful wife. Molly Van Horn was movie star beautiful, with a wide and lovely face that was full of warmth and without guile.

NEEDLESS TO SAY, I didn't go out for football or basketball. Although we know the truth (I was a lousy athlete and generally frightened of physical contact), I explained to Chris and anyone else who would listen that high school sports were for chumps and what this high school needed was a dose of Big Hugo. Big Hugo, I said, would straighten this place out in a hurry.

It was right about here that the big turning point in my life came, and I remember every detail.

Our high school was called Teachers College High School because it was part of the huge Eastern Illinois State Teachers College. One day I was walking across the college campus when P. J. Van Horn grabbed me by the arm and pulled me across the street into the Little Campus Coffee Shop and sat me down in a booth. He pulled out an enormous handkerchief, wheezed a great wheeze, spat into his handkerchief, and said, "You're chicken, Reynolds. You're too chicken to go out for football."

It was a preemptive strike, P. J. Van Horn had called in the helicopters. I was stunned, backing off into my corner of the booth, terrified of this coughing machine who had never spoken to me before but had peeked inside my heart with a single sentence.

I burbled something like, "I . . . I'm not chicken."

"Well," he said, softening considerably, "why don't we find out? Practice is at four o'clock, on the big field."

And without another word, he got up out of the booth and went out the door of the Little Campus, leaving behind a busted-up Beverly Reynolds.

Our football field was surrounded by a quarter-mile black cinder track, which was, in turn, surrounded by a great stand of oak trees. At four o'clock that afternoon, I was skulking in those trees staring at my shoes with my hands shoved deep down in my pockets when Coach Van Horn saw me and called me over.

"Beverly!" he boomed, "you're gonna play left tackle. Herbie'll take you to the locker room and get you suited up."

Herbie was Herbie Bickle, another oddball Coach Van Horn had collected, and the coach right away knew that Herbie was going to be my "bridge" back into the civilized world. So the two misfits walked to the gymnasium.

"I played a little football at Taft," I lied. "We were all-conference," whatever the hell that meant.

Herbie was not impressed, especially when I put the rib pads on backward.

Out on the practice field, I was at first mortified by how awkward I was. But by the time it was twilight and we had been through a dozen practice drills, blocking and tackling, I began to feel a strange new exhilaration. Herbie and I banged into each other (we weren't allowed to touch the ball, we were clearly foot soldiers), and I actually had a small shiver of self-respect run through me after I had made an acceptable tackle of Big Dave Scruggs, our fullback.

Big Dave was Big Hugo gone straight. He didn't have Big Hugo's filthy mouth or Big Hugo's entourage, and he was damn near blind, wearing these thick black rubber goggles when he played football. But he was tall and very brave and generally knocked everybody down when he charged out of the backfield on a running play. So my tackle of Big Dave got some attention, and my status as a pariah at Teachers College High School began to change.

Don't get me wrong, I was a terrible football player. The only time I got to play regular that first year was in the Villa Grove game when the first string left tackle, Bob Jones, was suspended for drinking beer.

But I was on the football team and Herbie Bickle was on the football team and P. J. Van Horn smiled and lied about our athletic gifts as he watched the two of us blunder about, disgracing the sport.

God knows how many other young men, stumbling around in the dark of adolescence, were helped by Coach Van Horn. And football was just the beginning. When he saw that I was a lousy football player, he edged me toward becoming the team "manager" who, in those days, was the guy who taped up your feet and made sure all the helmets got loaded on the bus. Now *there* was something I could do. Although I still suited up for every game, which kept my macho standing in place, I began to make a real, constructive contribution to the team as its manager.

And then basketball season came around. If I was lousy at playing football, I *really* stunk up the joint in basketball. I was very nearsighted so I couldn't see the basket properly, and since I had no natural talent the school certainly wasn't going to spring for another set of rubber goggles.

So during the basketball season, I was the full-time manager, which meant that I got to go to all the road games, sitting up front next to coach Van Horn, who drove the bus. For some reason, those long drives early in the evening and late at night are fixed forever in my memory. Because the coach had such terrible bronchitis, he had to roll down the window every few miles to spit out the phlegm in his throat, and a trail of white stuff streaked back across the bus windows on the left side. I suppose it was disgusting, but that's not the way I remember it. I remember it as something that made this great mound of a man touchingly real and vulnerable.

I don't know when P. J. Van Horn's trouble with the school administration began, but I remember that there were lots of people, including several of the better players on the football and basketball teams, who blamed the coach for our terrible won-lost record. We were, in fact, losing most all of the time.

I remember how wonderful it was on the rare occasion when we won.

By the way, P. J. Van Horn *wanted* to win as much as anybody. I especially remember the morning after we beat Paris, Illinois, in a close basketball game. I went to the gym and found it all decorated with our school colors, bright blue and yellow crepe paper streamers. A huge cardboard sign had been plastered on one of the basketball backboards that said, "Congratulations TC High Basketball Team! TC 68, Paris 66!" It turned out that after we won that game, P. J. Van Horn and his beautiful wife Molly had spent most of the night Scotchtaping up streamers and decorating the gym to surprise us at practice the next day.

IT'S FUNNY HOW you can put things together later in life. I remember being pretty happy in early 1946. We had won the war and my family came home in a 1938 Packard and I was glad to see them. P. J. Van Horn's understanding of scared children had worked a magic change in me, but I had a lot of catching up to do. If only I had understood things better, I might have been able to help him when his troubles came.

Henry "Hank" Lucas was a veteran, and veterans ruled the world in those days. Hank had been hired by the college as assistant coach for all high school sports, and he arrived just in time for the start of the 1946 football season. As I recall it now, I was one of the jerks who fell hook, line, and sinker for Hank Lucas's new approach to the game. Hank saw himself as a warrior and was disgusted by P. J. Van Horn's casual approach to the game.

"Fundamentals! Fundamentals!" he would shout during practice as he encouraged us to break up each other's bodies in a series of tackling and blocking drills that were more like bayonet practice.

And I, God help me, liked it. Lucas, faced with a football squad of sixteen in a game that fielded eleven players, decided to make Herbie Bickle and me into real football players in case somebody got hurt. P. J. Van Horn just looked on benignly. He really liked Hank Lucas and let him take over the football squad. But Hank didn't notice or thank him, he just pounded into our heads the commandments of fundamentals and the sacrament of winning. Herbie and I slammed into the tackling dummy a thousand times that summer. As tackles, we learned about how you fill the hole when the guard pulls out, and we were all tuned up to come in a game to give the real football players some rest.

But Hank Lucas was not a nice man.

Over at the Little Campus, surrounded by his favorite players, Hank criticized P. J. Van Horn, ridiculed his "soft" approach to the game and even made veiled references to the fact that Coach Van Horn had not served his country in the recent war. Fact is, P. J. Van Horn was 4F because of his bronchitis, and as far as I'm concerned he served his country very well during those years as a kind man in an fitful world.

P. J. Van Horn's moment of truth came in the last game of the 1946 season, the game against Charleston High School.

Each year, our football season ended with a game against Charleston High School. It was a scary game. CHS was not just another high school; it was our "townie" high school, where the regular working-class folks of Charleston, Illinois, sent their children. The rivalry was ugly, between the smart-assed kids of Teachers College High, most of us connected to the college, and the tougher sons and daughters of farmers, merchants, and working people at CHS.

TC had a terrific football season in 1946. We won half our games! It was a direct result of Hank Lucas's work ethic. In a single season, he had transformed us into a mean, snarling bunch of blue-and-yellow-suited soldiers who screamed in the locker room, prayed in the huddle, and committed felony assault on the field.

P. J. Van Horn didn't complain, although I thought I saw a sadness in his eyes, kind of like the look of the people on the train after the president had died. Coach Van Horn actually sat in the stands that year, leaving the bench to Hank Lucas and his sixteen felons.

Everybody in town came to the CHS-TC game.

Traditionally, CHS beat the hell out of us. It was an annual therapy for the folks downtown who thoroughly detested all of the college people and their offspring. But this year it was different. From the opening whistle we really socked 'em, and by halftime the score was 14 to 7 in our favor. (Honesty compels me to report that Herbie Bickle, picking up a fumble when playing defense, ran the length of the field for a touchdown, and although I slapped him on the back and shook his hand, I was murderously jealous.)

At halftime, I looked up at P. J. Van Horn in the stands. He was sitting next to Molly with a huge blanket wrapped around the both of them. The coach smiled when we locked eyes and gave me a thumbs-up, which for some reason ran a thrill through me like a mountain stream.

Dave Scruggs, our fullback, was magnificent that day. He gained almost a hundred yards in the first half. But on the first play of the third quarter, Dave was coldcocked by one of the CHS linebackers and was suddenly lying on the ground, his rubber glasses cockeyed and his eyes rolling back into his head. His body seemed to me to be convulsing at first, but he quickly recovered and was back on his feet and back in the huddle.

P. J. Van Horn was out of stands and onto the field in a second. I especially remember the look of anguish on his face as he lumbered out into the middle of the field, put his arm around Dave Scruggs, and walked him out of the huddle and onto the bench.

Hank Lucas was livid. He started screaming, "What the hell do you think you're doing, Van Horn?"

P. J. Van Horn didn't take his eyes off David Scruggs as he answered, "I'm taking this boy out of the game. He's going to the hospital."

"He's what?" Lucas was apoplectic.

Van Horn hardly heard him. He rolled David's eyelid back. "Yes," he said, "to the hospital."

A year of anger poured out of Hank Lucas, "You pansy son of a bitch, who do you think you are! This is no boy, this is a man! And he's gonna play this game!"

We were winning! For the first time in a hundred years, we were beating CHS, and P. J. Van Horn was going to take our best player away from us. I'm afraid that part of me was on Hank Lucas's side.

P. J. Van Horn slipped his arm around Dave's shoulders and the two of them began to walk off the field.

Hank Lucas did the only thing he knew how to do, he smashed P. J. Van Horn in the face with a roundhouse right, and Coach Van Horn went down like a tree, dragging Dave Scruggs with him. The two of them were all scrambled together when I heard a familiar sound: P. J. Van Horn was having a coughing fit. The great handkerchief came out of his pocket like a white flag, and all of us, including Hank Lucas, backed off, waiting for the coughing and the spitting to subside. When it was over, P. J. Van Horn and David Scruggs got to their feet and with some considerable dignity walked on the black cinder track all the way to the end of the field and disappeared into the trees.

We lost the game. CHS slaughtered us 35 to 14.

More important, Dave Scruggs was released from the hospital within a half hour. There was nothing wrong with him except a lump on the right eyebrow. But there was no forgiving Coach Van Horn who had removed Dave from the field of play. The college alumni association, which had forced the hiring of Hank Lucas in the first place, rose up and demanded that P. J. Van Horn be fired.

He wasn't fired exactly, he just sort of disappeared, in stages, after Christmastime, like Santa Claus.

And I never got to thank him.

Overture and Beginners

THERE IS NOTHING wrong with the way I was raised. My mother may have laid the Catholic frosting on a bit thick, but then a forbidding God was general issue during the Second World War. He glued things back together when they blew apart, and you simply didn't have time to run around finding out if he existed. You might get shot and go to hell by the time the argument was settled.

Not that I was a soldier, mind you; I was just a kid who was born on Columbus Day in 1930, which made me fourteen when the war ended. For years I was of the opinion that my father had ignored me while my mother poisoned me with religion. I must have been pretty old before I figured out that they had given me what my friend Lefty used to call "a good malt base," by which he meant a couple of bottles of 3.2 beer before you started your serious drinking.

As you will soon see, it is not peculiar that I use booze as my principal figure of speech.

The sovereignty of the war and my family gave my life a steady course, and once I had passed through puberty and the war was over, I was prepared to live a small-potato life in Charleston, Illinois, a life that would have stretched from the rich alluvial black soil north of town to the arid farms in the south.

After all, I lived in the heartland, on what H. L. Mencken correctly called the "Chicago Palatinate." If there was a place in America where the pain and gold stars of depressions and wars are felt first and most keenly, it was right there in Coles County, Illinois, where I began.

But I didn't stay there, and this is the story about how the world and I changed, unfolded, blew up after I left home.

You see, my grandmother gave me some money, so I went to a fancy college, a crazy college. I got admitted with the help of a wonderful Virgil scholar named Kevin Clemmons. Mr. Clemmons was a whole epic of man all by himself, a defrocked priest back in the days when defrocking was right up there with treason and murder. But Mr. Clemmons had married and ended up working with my father in our little Teachers College in Charleston. People never quite understood why my nine-novenas-a-year Catholic mother never tried to run Kevin Clemmons out of town, but *I* understood, and you can begin to take the measure of this wonderful woman when you consider her easy social embrace of the apostate Clemmons and her later tolerance of me when I swapped God for whiskey. Mom ran her campaign to save Mr. Clemmons and me quietly in marathon prayer sessions down at St. Charles Borromeo Catholic Church.

Someday we'll see who was right, won't we?

So Kevin Clemmons knew someone at Antioch College in Yellow Springs, Ohio, and wrote a letter on my behalf. The next thing I knew I was sitting on the top bunk in a men's dormitory of the strangest place on earth.

Within seconds after I arrived, I began to change from a regular, civilized young Catholic penitent into a madcap radical staring into a new bright sun as the scales dropped from my eyes. Splat! went Francisco Franco. Zap! went the Holy Trinity. Plunk! went premarital abstinence.

Let the good times roll.

Antioch was and is a marmalade of educational ideas cooked up by Horace Mann. For example, you don't go to school all year round. You spend half the year on a "co-op" job in Bloomingdale's in New York City or some such place. The whole system is based on an "it's your nickel, kid" theory of education, an honor system in which such things as class attendance, personal behavior, and academic discipline are entirely up to you. Even the college bookstore had an unattended cash register. The only piper that had to be paid showed up in your final year when they added up your credits to see if you had enough to graduate. (In my final year I discovered that I had not taken a single physical education course. So I had to stuff rock climbing, calisthenics, basketball, camping I, camping II, swimming, and archery into my last semester. It damn near killed me.)

In a nod to conventional education, Antioch suggested that you spend your first full year on campus. That was when I discovered the theater. The theater at Antioch was like a chicken heart that gobbled me up. Down at the old Yellow Springs Opera House an irresistible mix of teachers, students, and professional actors from New York sailed the seven seas from Ben Jonson to George Abbott. We visited the battlefields of the fifteenth century, followed Tennessee Williams into the steamy South, sang the songs of *Of Thee I Sing* and *The Mikado* as loud as we could. We stopped by the ports and politics of Eugene O'Neill, Clifford Odets, and Paul Vincent Carroll. We learned about wars won and lost, women spirited away, and uncovered secrets, long entombed.

I was overwhelmed, transported, mesmerized. I became a carpenter, a bit player, a stage manager; I climbed the highest masts, built palaces, and learned of love. It was nothing to work through the night, slapping "dutchmen"— long strips of cloth soaked with paint and glue—on the cracks between the flats that became the bulkheads of *The Hairy Ape* or the walls of an Irish peasant cottage in *The Wise Have Not Spoken*.

And then there was liquor. I had my first-ever drink at the opening night party of *The Glass Menagerie*.

Liquor wasn't around much when I was back home in Charleston. Oh, maybe one Wednesday a month my father would have too many beers at the Social Science Department poker game, and there was always an argument when he got home. But my mother had better reasons to be terrified of booze; her father was an alcoholic who died under the steel wheels of a Washington, D.C., streetcar. During the war, when we lived for a while in Washington, Mom took me on an educational tour of the family graveyard. In the center stood a tall obelisk with names engraved from top to bottom.

"Cirrhosis of the liver, cirrhosis of the liver, cirrhosis of the liver," she repeated as she pointed to each name in turn.

So when I took my first drink, a beer, at *The Glass*

Menagerie party, all of those neglected genes woke up and cheered, danced in my head, and informed me that the world was perfect, all women were beautiful, and that I was very wise beyond my years.

Within the space of a year I had raced away from my past and jumped into this pond of anarchy with a glad cry. Everything was fresh and new, and all the great questions rained down from heaven, making a terrible flood that washed away my soil, my town, my farms . . . my little history. It was very complicated. There was no God, the Rosenbergs were being murdered, and T. S. Eliot was a fascist who could write poetry. I spun from one epiphany to the next, almost like moving through the Stations of the Cross seeking absolution at each stop for my behavior at the one before. And on all of this, I floated on a sea of booze, the great resolver of chords, the arbiter of intellect.

And I sat above it all, on a tall stool with a glass of whiskey in one hand and a hammer in the other. I was smart enough to feel the loss and pain, but I had the perfect anesthetic and a plan to rebuild the world.

Then there were gentler times, moments of real learning and grace. I remember, for example, the morning when I learned for the second time how to listen to classical music. (Back in Charleston, my friend Mrs. Trimble had taught me Beethoven, but all of that was drowned in a bucket of beer.)

I woke up hungover in the apartment of an Antioch senior who had taken pity on me when I was homeless the night before. He was listening to Bach's B Minor Mass when I opened my eyes. My aching head and recently acquired atheism made this hymn to God a noisy business despite the fact that it was Sunday morning.

He saw I was in pain, turned off the record, and asked me if I would like to learn how to listen to music.

"Why not?"

"You must listen to a single instrument," he said, "the flutes in the orchestra behind the chorus, for example. You try to hear only the flutes, threading their way through all the other sound, and the music will reveal itself."

He put the record back on and I squinted my eyes and tried to listen to the flutes. It was a smallish miracle. Walking along the rope of the flutes, great assonant chords followed one another until the entire Mass consumed me. I had been to Mass a million times with my mother and nothing like this had ever happened.

AT CHRISTMASTIME, MY parents were properly appalled when I arrived home a hitchhiking, raggedy Beverly who couldn't stop talking.

"Where's the forty dollars I sent you for the bus fare?" asked my father.

"In here," I lied, pointing at my head, "the Random House edition of *Remembrance of Things Past.*"

The truth is that to this day I have not read *Remembrance of Things Past.* At Antioch it quickly became my practice to memorize a few obscure passages from great literary works, passages that I could drop on Audrey Sellmer with the perfect body late at night in the Old Trail Tavern. I quickly covered the entire canon of English literature this way, quoting extensively, for example, from *Timon of Athens*, the one Shakespearean play I figured nobody, not even the teachers, knew.

Maybe I'm being a little hard on myself. I *did* hear all the plays that we performed; I had to, I was usually standing just off stage at the switchboard. And I loved the "short" arts, poetry and painting, that could be taken in at a glance. But woe to Milton, Dante, Byron, and the like with their long, hilly narratives. Eliot, Dickinson, and Roy Campbell were more my style, perfect for instant wisdom and seduction.

I have never been able completely to shake this old fraud of mine. Even today, when reading *A Farewell to Arms*, I find myself studying the book jacket for a synopsis and automatically skimming the text. I can't even let the plain-spoken Hemingway have his say.

WELL, CHRISTMAS OF 1949 was soon over, and wouldn't you know that I next popped, like a cork, out of the Christopher Street stop of the New York City subway. A year and one semester had passed and I was on my first co-op job.

I remember *everything* about that first minute in the city, standing under the old ornate Victorian subway entrance on Sheridan Square in Greenwich Village with its elaborate newstand and kiosk. I was wearing a funny-looking fur-lined canvas jacket with hood that my mother had given me, and it was in that very minute that I decided that I would live there, exactly there, for the rest of my life.

I checked into my job far uptown as a salesman in Bloomingdale's book department, the perfect job for the old faker, skimmer, quoter from Yellow Springs. I had forgotten to bring a suit to New York and so I borrowed one from my roommate who was a full foot shorter than me. Thus I circled through the best-sellers and remainders at Bloomingdale's in a pair of pants with the crotch at knee level.

We right away found an apartment, on West Fifteenth Street between Seventh and Eighth avenues. It was a basement railroad flat, which meant that our three little rooms were in a row, like passenger cars. We were right next to the furnace, and once a month, on Wednesday, a load of coal was dumped in the hallway blocking our front door, so we had to hole up with a two-gallon jug of red wine for two days.

Bloomingdale's just didn't understand prolonged absences, and I was fired.

That was fine with me because I was having trouble squeezing my job into my royal progress through the bars of Greenwich Village. Each day I stopped at the Riviera, the San Remo, Minetta's (for a sandwich), and finally Louie's. Wonderful, wonderful Louie's, tucked into Sheridan Square across the street from Cafe Society Downtown. Louie's had a bartender named Red and was filled with the likes of me, gobbling kids strutting our stuff, writing poetry on napkins, and lining up companions for the rest of the night.

Once in a while an actual published writer would show up. I remember Frederick Buchener and Dylan Thomas by name. They held court in the left-hand back booth. When I was introduced to Mr. Thomas he threw up on my mother's canvas jacket with the hood.

But my immediate future was at the other end of the bar. There sat Jorge Cervantes, a strangely graceful, dark-haired man who talked rapid-fire English in a glamorous Spanish accent, interspersing "you know" as a replacement for the words he hadn't learned. He was a stage director from Panama who had his own special vision. He had swallowed Konstantin Stanislavsky whole. Jorge argued passionately for the "method," an acting formula in which the actor uses his own life and experience as the port of entry into a charac-ter. Both the European and radical American theater had el-evated Stanislavsky to almost sacramental status. Jorge, with the "method" in his knapsack, wanted to start his own the-ater, away from Broadway, steeped in the psychodrama of his actors.

I sat on the bar stool next to him and fought him tooth and nail. Here I was, a man who had just got in from the theater in Yellow Springs, where I had visited the seven seas, spent a year in the fifteenth century, in New Orleans, in the hold of the S.S. *Glencairn*, the drawing rooms of Europe. How could I jam my own little shabby small-town history into all of that magic stuff?

An actor, as I saw it, becomes somebody else, a brooding Cassius, a frail Amanda Wingfield, a lunatic Harry Binion in *Room Service*. Great acting, I announced in my cups, was an act of craft not a spasm of recall!

But as time would tell, and the whole world would know one day, Jorge was right and I was drunk . . . and wrong.

Aside from my fatuous opinions about the art of acting, I was exactly what Jorge needed as winter turned toward spring that year and Bloomingdale's sent me packing. Jorge was slowly gathering a group of Village vagabonds around him. My contribution was as a "technician," an extremely imprecise craft in those days. The ability to plug in a spotlight, jury-rig a dimmer, or paint a line on a flat that looked like real wainscoting from the fifth row of the orchestra was more than sufficient to convince our Panamanian *infante* that I was useful. I was particularly valuable to him because I did *not* want to be an actor and was thus free of the silly, shallow ego that comes with that line of work.

So, over the spring of 1950, we gathered by the Hudson River.

First came Andy Alp, the cartoonist with the busy, flashing, frantic eyes. He drew a successful syndicated cartoon strip called "Millie the Talker," and it was a terrible burden to him. His deadlines followed him around like dark ghosts and made the light in his eyes disappear when he talked about how much he hated Millie and her vain and stupid life with balloons coming out of her mouth.

Then came Portia and Kathleen, mother and ingenue, a lesbian couple who hung out at the Purple Place where where I would sit, from time to time, and indulge a strange arousal as I watched the women dance together.

There was Eddie Marsh, the dancer, who moved through all of his life like an elegant inchworm.

And I mustn't forget old Roger Rafferty. He was the master key to the whole thing. Roger couldn't *do* anything as far as I could tell, but he had some money, and Jorge was always having secret conversations with him, conversations that seemed to stop abruptly whenever I came by. I remember him especially because Roger was older, and he was all we had by way of parenting in this little antipode of children.

We called ourselves The Loft Players because Roger had found us a loft above a plastics factory where we set about the business of rehearsing and making the props for our first production. I remember yelling at rehearsals over the crazy racket of the factory, but I also remember Andy Alp's great joy when he first arrived with a roll of chicken wire and a bucket of wet plaster to make the masks.

The choice of our first play was the first evidence of Jorge's natural genius. Somewhere, somehow, we were going to put on a production of *Alice in Wonderland.*

It was a wonderful and brazen choice. At first I wondered what Stanislavsky would think of the bunch of us running around in papier-mâché headpieces pretending to be rabbits and dormice. But then I saw that *Alice in Wonderland* was the story of our new lives. It was clear to me that just outside of Charleston, Illinois, somewhere near Ashmore, on my way to college, I had fallen down the rabbit hole.

As we all had fallen down our rabbit holes.

And when we stopped falling we had abandoned the loft and were all tumbled together into the middle of a dark forest where there lived poets and viola players, anarchists and birds.

I'm telling the truth.

It was called the Maverick Estate, and it was in this black, piney woods outside of Woodstock, New York, that we found ourselves. Once upon a time somebody named Maverick had died and left an enormous track of densely wooded land for the use of artists of all sorts.

Because the woods were so deep and dark, you couldn't tell that they were buzzing with amateur poets and painters, sometimes living a few hundred yards away from fancy scholars and prose writers of all sorts. But very late at night, if you squinted hard and listened, you could hear old typewriters clacking away and almost see their poems and stories emerging from the trees.

At the center of this black forest of the arts was the Maverick Theatre, a great old ramshackle barn built from rough-sawed twelve-inch pine boards, which surrounded what seemed to us (as we had just left a tiny loft on Twenty-third Street) to be an enormous, echoing chamber with a large proscenium stage and four hundred chairs.

I must immediately tell you that even as we arrived,

Greenwich Village tilted on its side and dumped a covey of drunks and pretenders into Woodstock. Most of them were dispatched to the Sea Horse Bar at the far end of town, where they drank Green Hornets, a poisonous concoction made by mixing crème de menthe and gin.

Two of these hangers-on were a marvelous, legendary pair—Jack Stockbridge and Louie Weber. Jack claimed to have fought with the Abraham Lincoln Brigade in the Spanish Civil War and would tell tales of heroes and political faction fights at the slightest provocation, while Louie, an enormous Mexican-German, told hilarious stories about how he and his twin brother switched beds and girls and could be told apart only by a very small hammer and sickle tattooed on his brother's dick that became a flag at full mast when aroused.

Jack and Louie were both painters, billboard sign painters that summer, and Jack would make up revolutionary songs like "Our Backs Against the Wall at Barcelona" as they smoked excellent hashish and teetered on the scaffolding while painting full-length portraits of fourteen-foot-high brown-breasted ladies cavorting alongside Route 212.

I was, after all, nineteen years old and it was all very wonderful.

Back in the forest, the rehearsals for *Alice in Wonderland* went forward. In addition to my regular jobs as the technical director, electrician, and carpenter, I was to play the part of the Mad Hatter. This entitled me to wear Andy Alp's masterpiece, an enormous papier-mâché head with a top hat on it with a sign saying, IN THIS STYLE, "10/6." Jorge immediately decided that I needed a distinctive walk, and top-heavy though I was, I produced a ridiculous ducked-toed gait that made everybody laugh. It looked like this:

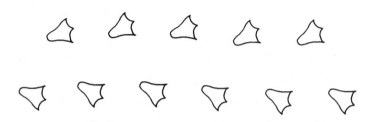

"Perfect," said Jorge, "but we've got to motivate it."

"Got to what?" I asked.

"Motivate it," said Jorge, exasperated. "You are crossing a stream, back home. There's a rock there, and there, and there," he added, making chalk circles on the floor of the stage. "Now, cross that stream!"

I crossed the stream and it looked like this:

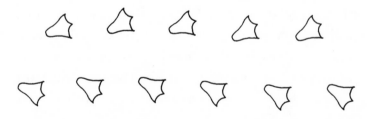

So I poured a little tea on the nose of the Dormouse.

Needless to say, I was continuously in love. At first, I was in love with Maude Gozy, who had introduced me to sex in Titsworth Hall at Sarah Lawrence College. Maude was a mannish sort of lady whom I invited to be my technical assistant at the Maverick. She lasted about two weeks into the season until a puddle of leather arrived one afternoon on a large motorcycle, and my first love disappeared in a noisy, smoky cloud.

And then there was Lois Kallen, sweet and skinny and smart. Lois lived in the actual town of Woodstock, which was, in those days, a collection of smart shops and a very fancy professional theater where Eva Le Gallienne played Saint Joan and was burned at the stake each night. My friend Lois Kallen was stricken with a form of diabetes for which there was no cure. But she had a great kindness in her and saw to it that I had an occasional clean shirt that summer and good book to read and think about.

She died the next December. I received a Christmas card that said good-bye.

I slept most nights on a hay bale in a little shed next to the theater. I was, after all, the technical director and responsible for the safety of the house. Of course, there wasn't a whole lot to rob, unless you knew a pawnshop that would give you money for old floppy flats, an ancient electrical rheostat switchboard, and a great pile of papier-mâché heads depicting hatters, queens and kings, dormice, griffins, mock turtles, and a Cheshire cat.

I woke up each morning around eleven with a thundering headache. On one morning, late in June, just before the grand opening of *Alice in Wonderland,* my father arrived driving a 1939 Packard.

That's right, my father, Samuel Taylor Reynolds, distinguished professor of political and social science, at Eastern Illinois State Teachers College, arrived at our little Roman festival having driven 948 miles to visit his youngest son.

It happened that that was the morning that Eddie Marsh had decided to cover himself with olive oil and dance stark naked to Vivaldi's *Four Seasons.* The outside stage door was wide open, and my father was treated to either Summer, Winter, Spring, or Fall.

After a grim little wave to me as I fell off my hay bale and out of my shed, my father shoved the old floorboard stick shift into reverse, and the Packard roared backward down the Old Maverick Road in a great plume of dust and noise.

In the family, the matter never came up.

Threading throughout this story, like the flutes in the B Minor Mass, is a rope of anarchy. None of us were warriors; we were more like infant anarchists. Most of us were children who had been born just a little too late to be either the victims or the perpetrators of William Butler Yeats's "blood-dimmed tide" that had devoured the first half of the century. Out there in the woods, loving and playacting, listening to poetry and playing croquet with flamingoes, we were the gathering recipe for the sixties to come.

Somehow we knew that there had been enough of governments, enough of dying.

Up on Overlook Mountain, not ten miles from the theater, lived an old man named Francis. Francis was a *real* anarchist, who flew a black flag and lived in a cave. Twice that summer, we found our way to his hole in the mountain, where he served us his homemade raisin wine and talked to us of Proudhon and Prince Kropotkin and the always-gathering storm. Up there on Overlook Mountain, listening to the old man rail about the tryanny of property and the injustice of government, I heard those grand assonant chords again and knew that whatever I was to become, anything was possible, that we all could make a new beginning.

But back down in the forest, at the theater, we had a problem.

We had run out of scenery, the stuff that was to transform the Maverick Theatre into Alice's Wonderland. Andy Alp and I had a solution. The rocks and trees and mushrooms could be made with four-ply cardboard, a magical medium that could be cut with a frisket knife and bent into the shape of griffons and hedgehogs and forests that moved mysteriously across the back of the stage. What we needed were huge four-foot-by-ten-foot sheets of the cardboard, the kind that was thick enough to paint without wrinkling and stand up without bracing.

Roger Rafferty announced that there was no more money in the till.

That night at the Sea Horse, Jack and Louie and I, smashed silly by a new shipment of hashish, sat in a dark corner of the saloon, our elbows on the table, cooking up a crime. Jack had a pickup truck and Louie knew a warehouse in New York that had the cardboard sheets we needed. A phone call arranged for an open door, and the three of us immediately piled into the truck and headed down the brand-new superhighway to the city. Jack drove and Louie and I sat in the back of the truck, screaming songs in harmony directly into the wind.

At two A.M. we drove into the city itself and we were silenced by the tall, dark buildings that surrounded us. At the warehouse, Jack backed into the loading dock. As promised, the door was open, and gently, soundlessly, we loaded twenty tall packs of four-ply cardboard sheets into the bed of the truck. Louie and I jammed into the front seat, Jack slipped the truck into gear, and we headed north.

The cardboard heist solved our scenery problem. In a week's time, mushrooms and movable trees, dodo birds and caterpillars filled the stage, and on the sixth of July 1950, in the middle of the mushrooms, in the middle of a great barn that was in the middle of the darkest forest west of Baden-Baden, we opened our play.

Admission was one dollar. If you didn't have a dollar, you could bring a steak or a dozen eggs. Roger Rafferty had dreamed up "barter night" so that we could feed the company with food used as the price of admission. Most people were generous with bushel baskets of unshucked summer corn or gallons of wine. Occasionally some deadbeat, probably from the end of the bar at the Sea Horse, stiffed us with a can of beans.

On opening night the audience came from all the world. Jack and Louie led a caravan of honking trucks and cars through the center of Woodstock, and Eddie Marsh set off some fireworks just as soon as it was dark so that the fancy folks in town saw two bright red bursting stars in the sky above the forest.

The curtain was scheduled for 8:45. By 8:30, the four hundred chairs were full and I had to admonish Jorge for an unprofessional peek through the curtain at the audience. Promptly at 8:45, I pulled the dimmer on the house lights, and the Queen of Hearts, who wasn't due on stage for quite a while, pulled the ropes to open the curtain.

I brought up the lights, and there sat Alice in a sea of stolen cardboard.

Andy Alp had outdone himself with great cranky trees and bright orange tulips on a stage steeped in the spooky and wonderful drawings of John Tenniel. A grand, long dining table was set out for the Tea Party. The Caterpillar lounged on his mushroom, smoking an enormous hookah. A sleepy Dormouse arrived with two thrones, one under each paw, and the Five, Six, and Seven of Diamonds played croquet with the Knave.

Offstage left I set all the dimmers, and Maude Gozy helped me into my Mad Hatter's head with the enormous hat. I scurried on stage, duckwalking, crossing the stream. Andy had cut eyeholes so I could see properly, but Maude had screwed the huge mask around crooked so I was as blind as a bat. During the thunderous applause that greeted the set and the costumes, I ran into the Mushroom and shouted at the Caterpillar to fix my head so I could see. Having no arms, the Caterpillar referred me to the Dormouse who, by standing on my feet and wrapping his hairy arms around my hat, gave me a mighty Dormouse of a twist that aligned my eyes with the eyeholes, and to the delight of the audience, I was free to duckwalk all the way across the stage to Alice. I elbowed the March Hare out of the way and sat at the banquet table to deliver my first line, which echoed six or seven times around inside of my mask.

"Your hair wants cutting," said I.

"You should learn not to make personal remarks," replied Alice. "It's very rude."

And we were off! The Griffon got some of his lines backward, and the Queen of Hearts, played by Frank McDonald, forgot who she was supposed to execute so she condemned the entire cast with a single sweep of her knuckly finger, "Off with her head! Off with his head! Off with *all* of their heads!" she pronounced in Frank's booming bass voice.

During the Lobster Quadrille, as the Mock Turtle, tears streaming down his shell, was singing " 'Will you walk a little faster?' said a whiting to a snail, 'There's a porpoise close behind us, and he's treading on my tail . . .'"

All of a sudden my headpiece was filled with the bright blue light of an electrical explosion and I could see through my eyeholes that a bright snake of fire was making its way from the switchboard toward the cardboard trees that lined the stage.

To everyone's astonishment, I stood on my head, jumped out of my hat, and ran bareheaded toward the fire. Jorge stood there with a broom in his hands, paralyzed with panic. Thank God, he panicked in Spanish.

"Fuego! Fuego! El bosque está quemado!" wailed Jorge, bravely beginning to wave his broom at the forest fire but actually fanning the flames.

Maude and I ran onto the stage, trying to topple the burning cardboard forest, but the fire had reached the masking curtains and streaked upward past the pinrail and into the loft.

Smoke billowed for the first time from the proscenium, and the audience began to stand. In the rear of the house, Roger Rafferty, who had been sorting steaks and counting ears of corn, took over. Opening the two huge barn doors in the back of the house, he politely announced, "If you'll step this way, ladies and gentlemen, refreshments will be served while we put out the fire."

Roger Rafferty had no idea what possessed him to say it, but the effect was masterful. It appears the Alice madness had captured everyone. The audience quickly and silently filed out of the theater, which was just beginning to burn like a great campfire. In no more than five minutes, the flames were leaping upward as the old dry pine boards on all sides burst into great yellow flames reaching for the sky.

All of the actors and Maude and I ran out the stage door. Thus a big bowl of motley, a tossed salad of griffins and hatters, caterpillars and decks of cards, tumbled onto the ground next to the theater. We were a like a garland around Jorge, who sat there with the beautiful red and yellow flames reflecting in the flood of his tears.

It was the perfect place and the perfect night for miracles. The audience surrounded the building, standing farther and farther away as the fire grew hotter. Some were protecting the forest from the burning embers. The grown-ups grabbed sticks and branches to push the burning shards back toward the fire. The children, who had come to visit Alice in Wonderland, climbed the pine trees to break off the little tree limbs that might ignite.

Jack and Louie stood at the center of it all, shouting orders and directing operations, spraying water from our only hose onto the forest, and when it was clear that there was nothing else to do but watch the old gray building burn, we all began to sing.

It was one grand chorus of "The Battle Hymn of the Republic," a song everybody knew. There were four hundred and fifty voices singing "Mine eyes have seen the glory of the coming of the Lord," and it seemed that we all had joined some stream of history as the music soared upward, mixed with the loud crackle of the fire as we saw a burning cardboard mushroom fly away.

It was the beginning, not the end.

The next morning, as we rubbed our eyes and washed the cinders from our faces, the entire town of Woodstock seemed to appear on our doorstep. Jack and Louie had organized bulldozers, a backhoe, and dump trucks. An army of citizens dressed in their working clothes proceeded to clear away the rubble of the old theater.

The site was filled with hopeful faces. Andy Alp had lined up all the masks along the road and was rushing from one to another with a paintbrush in his hand. Even Jorge, who had retreated to his room the night before, appeared and was frantically rehearsing the play for an outdoor production, this time with the real forest as our backdrop.

We hardly missed a beat. In three days the audience returned and sat on the ground and watched me duckwalk over to Alice, whack the March Hare, and announce as rudely as I could, "Your hair wants cutting!"

We performed seven plays that summer, each a little deeper than the last as Jorge began to catch the tempo of the time and the promise of our generation. Stanislavsky won the day.

It was, I think, the first real summer of the flowers. Eighteen years later, the summer ended on the streets of Chicago. And in between, a great civil rights movement had taken a new measure of the land.

Oh, yes, wars were fought, but with fewer patriots and without conviction.

And I had been there, washed out of Illinois into a new river where most everything was changed, especially the way we looked at one another. However drunk, however selfish, and however silly or obscene, there was the scent of Camelot.

For just that little while, the smell of love was in the air.

My Primrose Path

I *LIKED THE* army. Sue me. I liked the company of men. I liked the smell of cold ale in the barracks. I even liked the end of a fourteen-mile march, full pack and high adrenaline. I should tell you that the army I was in from September of 1953 to September of 1955 didn't shoot anybody on purpose. The Korean War had settled into the Pamunjom peace talks, which, as far as I know, are still going on. I had avoided the whole goddamn war by going to college, thank you. I am probably a pacifist and I am certainly a coward.

But I liked the army. I liked the feel of it, I liked wearing the same color clothes every day and I got to meet guys like Anton LeBeaux. Anton was one of the great men in my life. He's stuck on my hard palate like chewing gum and I can't lick him loose.

I'll tell just one Anton LeBeaux story. In the days right after the Korean War, it wasn't easy to get guys to join the army. So they had this "re-enlistment bonus" in which you got six thousand dollars if you "re-upped," that is, agreed to stay in the army for a couple more years after your time ran out. Anton, who drank ale in green bottles all day and all night (thus the smell in the barracks), needed a lot of money to stay afloat, so he went from army base to army base all over the country re-enlisting and picking up those six-thousand-dollar checks. This was in the days before computers, so they didn't catch up to him until long after he had spent the money. When I met him in Fort Monmouth, New Jersey, he was committed to serving his country for the next one hundred and twelve years.

Anyway, Fort Monmouth is just down the road from New York City, and I had worked a deal with my CO that gave me most weekends off. So I routinely went up to New York to visit my girlfriend, a beautiful young lady from Pottstown, Pennsylvania, who had once done me wrong.

One Friday afternoon when Miss Pottstown was in Pottstown, I was alone in her New York apartment when the phone rang and a sultry voice identified itself as a pal of Miss Pottstown, one Eve Preminger. Thus began an adventure that would, one way or another, occupy the next several years of my life.

That evening we met in a Blarney Stone saloon near Eve's apartment on the East Side of Manhattan. I remember that the Friday night fights were making a hell of a racket on television and that we looked into each other's eyes, experiencing a sort of beery triumph, a triumph that we had stumbled across something that wasn't complicated, something that required no lying or four-flushing, that meant we could do whatever happened next without worrying about whether or not we would ever be in love.

The lady from Pottstown was understandably upset when I told her about Eve, and she threw all my clothes out the third-story window of her apartment.

Eve had everything. She was short and pretty and smart and had been in a duck blind with Raymond Burr when she was younger.

On our second date I learned that Eve was a scion of the Preminger family, the movie Premingers.

The two brothers, Otto and Ingo, were very important. They had both escaped from Austria ahead of the Nazis. Ingo, Eve's father, had prospered as a Hollywood agent and producer. He was, and is, a fine fellow who strokes his chin. Otto, as all the world knows, was a famous director and a son of a bitch.

Both Otto and Ingo despised me. You have to see it from their point of view. Eve was their best shot, off-the-chart brilliant, the oldest of the children (Otto didn't have any kids until much later when he held a press conference to announce that he had fathered one of Gypsy Rose Lee's offspring). Their little "Eva" had hooked up with this rude, drunken Irish jerk who didn't know a first from a second banana.

The courtship was lush. I remember a lot of free booze and expensive hotel rooms with Otto humiliating perfectly nice people who had come to seek his favor. His mouth moved in a particularly obscene way, lots of gums and slobber, as he mowed down actors, screenwriters, anyone who was careless enough to pay court to him.

I must say he was very kind to Eve, which meant that he had to be civil to me. There were a couple of dinners at the Stork Club in the Cub Room, and I saw my first one-hundred-dollar bill when Otto paid the tab at Le Pavillon.

And I met Marilyn Monroe and I danced with Judy Garland.

So what am I complaining about?

At Sardi's the good seats are the booths and tables immediately to your left as you walk in. Anyplace else is for losers, supporting actresses, and tourists. You can bet Otto had us sitting in the good seats that afternoon when he leaned over and said to me, "Would you like to meet Marilyn Monroe?" I looked up and she was sitting two tables away from me. All I could see were her very white shoulders, nape, and upper back, which looked to me like John Locke's tabula rasa, where everything is new and without sin or flaw.

And then it got better.

At Otto's request, she stood up and slowly turned around and extended her hand toward me over the empty table that separated us. She was wearing an ivory gown that had been painted on her by Renoir himself; she got up that morning and said to Mr. Renoir, "Pierre Auguste, please paint me into my ivory gown so I can meet Beverly Reynolds today."

I said "How do you do," which was ridiculous because I knew that she did exceptionally well, and at the moment our eyes met, I had a religious experience. If anything had been wrong with me that day—a missing limb, a chill, an inoperable cancer—I would have been made whole in that instant and gone on to live as a monk, silent in the Swiss mountains.

Judy Garland was another matter. Before meeting Ms. Monroe, I had no preconceptions of her other than a wrinkly photograph in the barracks. But I had been a big fan of Judy Garland for several years. I had actually seen her at the Palace, sort of spilt over the front of the stage singing "Somewhere Over the Rainbow." She was heartbreakingly young and beautiful and wise in those days, with a powerful voice that seemed to sing in harmony with itself, reaching far up into the upper balcony where I sat enraptured. I had all her albums, including one called *Alone.* That was a sort of "Book of Judy," a touching series of song-psalms that explained the despairing parts of my life to me as only another alcoholic could.

Anyway, Eve and I were in Hollywood briefly for the opening night party of *Man With the Golden Arm* (one of those excellent novels that Otto dismembered). The party was in Romanoff's, and Ingo had bought me a blue tuxedo so I wouldn't disgrace the family. As I was trying to level my cummerbund, Eve suggested that I dance with Judy Garland. Before I could answer, I was swept into the arms of this very short, very fat, very drunk lady whose eyes were funny. We did a couple of turns and she was spun off into the arms of someone else and I was left alone to figure out a disgraceful, unfair world.

Meanwhile, back in the army, I was putting on plays in Fort Monmouth. We rolled back the Cinemascope screen so that it became a sky cyclorama and we turned Theatre One into the pillars of Rome for *Julius Caesar* and a French bedroom for Molière's *The Cheats of Scapin.* We actually toured *Caesar* to Fort Dix, which was, in those days a port of embarkation. I got an entire company of Puerto Ricans who were about to ship out to play the crowd. I was Cassius, and after I had stabbed Caesar and made my speech, I ran out front and cheer-led the crowd. They screamed Hispanic oaths as Brutus and Anthony "let slip the dogs of war."

By the way, for this army production, I mercilessly cut the play in half. I edited Shakespeare. What the hell, I was twenty-four years old.

Somehow, I got honorably discharged, and Eve and I got married in the apartment of Judge Sam Liebowitz in Brooklyn. Sam Liebowitz had been a brave and famous defense attorney but was an undistinguished "celebrity" judge who had married most of Hollywood, so he set us to giggling when he took us aside after the ceremony and explained that "none of my marriages has ever ended in divorce."

We went to the very small but perfect Tuscany Hotel on our wedding night, and we were off the next morning to Charleston, Illinois, to face the poorer (by far) half of the family, Dorothee and Samuel Taylor Reynolds. My mom demanded that we marry again in St. Charles Borromeo Catholic Church so that we wouldn't go straight to hell. This required the permission of Eve's parents, which we could never get, so we had a friend send a fake telegram to the Charleston priest granting permission. We were remarried "outside the rail" by Father Moriarty.

And the next week was heaven. We were alone. We had been besieged by everybody else's celebrity, so we set out to make up a life of our own. We set out, by the way, in a sky blue Kaiser sedan (which we called "Franz Joseph" after the Austrian emperor who had had so much trouble).

We moseyed west, pulling off into a Kansas pasture to make love, eating trout taken from the cold North Dakota streams, and down slantwise through the Rockies, taking the low road because the old Kaiser couldn't scramble up the mountains.

As I remember it, this marriage of ours was a little glade in the forest, a place where two very small rabbits sat very close together, spoke bunny language, and stole almost an entire year out of our regular lives. It was a precious year. Few people came to visit us in our San Francisco apartment where we ended up, and our trips to places like Hollywood were a waste of our very valuable time together. We were at the starting gate, neither willing to wrestle open the door of the world.

Once in a while we went to the movies, and we would become all the characters in the movie. We loved great and fancy fictional folks, whom we would bring home to our little forest place and serve tea and whiskey and consult with them about the way of the world.

We were proudly independent. Once, when we were driving Otto from the airport, he balled up a hundred-dollar bill and tossed it into my lap. I ate it.

We were, for a while, living on our own planet, complete and wonderful. But just outside, a thousand telephones and letters and relatives were ringing; everybody was demanding that we come on out and stop playing.

Then there came a time when we re-entered the world. I don't know why exactly; everyone does, I guess.

We flew back to New York City. We tried to bring the forest with us but there wasn't enough room on the airplane. I was mercy-booked into a job at United Artists films, and Eve went to law school.

Without the nourishing forest, the marriage began to falter. As everyone did in those days, we hired a consultant.

There was this lady named Mrs. Gladys who wrote a column in the New York *Daily News* advising people on emotional and marital matters. She was the "Dear Abby" of her time, with a somewhat higher-tone reputation as a professional and with letters after her name.

Anyway, simply *everyone* took his or her troubles to Gladys or her husband, whom I irreverently called "Mr. Gladys." He handled the overflow, including us.

When the good news spread around the Preminger clan that the Irish drunk was in trouble and the marriage was on the rocks, the smoke suddenly cleared and phone calls were made.

Now I'm not saying there was a fix, that Otto slipped Mr. Gladys a couple of house seats to come up with the correct recommendation. All I know is that when Eve and I got to his office, I got the distinct feeling I was playing out a prepared script. First, Mr. Gladys talked to both of us and then to me privately. I said I was pretty confused by the whole thing. I told him that the sex was terrific and that I drank too much but I loved my wife and was willing to sober up. I thought I had done great.

Then Eve had her private session. She must have been in his office for all of four minutes when they emerged, each with a powerfully sad and serious look.

"This marriage is over," announced Mr. Gladys, with the gravity of judge.

"Why?" I blubbered. Once, when I was very young, I went hunting with a shotgun because somebody told me to. A little rabbit popped up in front of me and I blew him into a thousand pieces. It was a terrible thing I had done and I honestly believe I have never done anything like it since. But Mr. Gladys had a shotgun too, and there were pieces of rabbit all over that room.

No one has ever answered my question. I was left to imagine what had been said in the four-minute meeting between Mr. Gladys and Eve. It could have been anything, like, "I don't love him anymore," or, more likely, "How long should we stay in here?" Mr. Gladys, fingering the house seats in his pocket, knew what to do.

So that was that. I got a divorce in Alabama, and Eve finished law school, married extremely well, had two daughters, and became a distinguished judge.

From time to time over the years, Eve and I have had rapturous lunches. We have always been able to go walking in our forest at will, and we can make each other laugh, I mean *laugh*, enough to turn heads and suggest scandal.

After the divorce, I went to Cuba. Sounds pretty adventurous nowadays, but the year was 1958 and Fidel Castro was still up in the hills above Santiago de Cuba preparing to pounce. I went to Havana to get drunk and mourn my marriage in the final hours of Batista's regime. It was the end of the Roman Empire: sex and booze, some raw Fundador brandy, and somebody's daughter in a sling chair. Havana was a dawn-to-dawn orgy with firecrackers, castanets, and opium. I remember the lottery kiosks and the whorehouses where a young woman's body and the American dollar were a lot sounder currency than the grungy peso. I ran with the cab drivers, who drove me from one madness to another, until, exhausted and filled with brandy, I took an old bus east to Santiago to try to find the revolution.

I had three bottles of Fundador in my poke and was thoroughly crocked by the time the bus spat me out in Santiago. I was insane. Somehow I found an old sugar farmer with a horse and a wagon. I gave him the rest of my money and said, "Find Fidel," as I collapsed in the back of his wagon and went sound asleep as we bumped along a mountain road.

I woke up back in the bus station in Havana. It came back to me slowly. The old man had endured my slobbering insults and had decided that this drunken Yankee was not fit for an audience with the Cuban redeemer and had loaded me onto the next bus heading west, stuffing my money back into my pocket. When I woke up I was soaked with piss and shame. There was nothing noble or brave to report. The revolution was in the heart of the old man and needed no help from me.

Back home, I discovered that I still had a job at United

Artists. Otto had forgotten to get me fired when I left the family.

I stayed on for years at United Artists, attempting to drink two different saloons dry. I could usually make it all the way to lunch without taking a drink, and then it was time for Beefeater martinis and hot antipasto at Luigi's, a mob joint around the corner from my job. I *loved* Luigi's. I was told that after the mobster summit at Appalachia was blown, the wiseguys repaired to the second-floor banquet room at Luigi's to divvy up the country. Occasionally, Carlo Gambino would drop by for lunch, and I was reliably told that Max the bartender was a hit man who murdered people after work each day.

My other stop, usually in the evening, was Jim Downey's, the only respectable establishment between Forty-fourth and Forty-fifth streets on Eighth Avenue. It was filled front to back with actors, an entire generation of young men and women all of whom would later be consumed by television, leaving me behind. Many of them were sobbing at the bar in those days, quoting that infamous statistic that "98 percent of the members of Actors Equity were unemployed in their own profession."

Since I had a regular job in the movie business, these guys put up with my sappy monologues about the "vacancy of the American theater" or other such nonsense. I was still the fast-mouthed dilettante who knew just a little bit about everything and when pushed to the wall would reach down like a gunslinger and whip out a quote from *Timon of Athens*. It *still* worked.

Between drinks, I was (God knows why) promoted to assistant publicity manager of United Artists Corporation. We released about forty films a year, most of them B pictures that got a lick and a promise from our department, but five or so of the pictures we distributed each year were multimillion-dollar, usually ghastly, extravaganzas that required a lot of promotion. Early on, we had released a film called *Sweet Smell of Success*, a slick little movie by Ernest Lehman that told the story of a Broadway columnist with a heart of pewter who did terrible things to perfectly nice people. In the course of publicizing that movie, I did a little, very little, research into the history of publicity stunts in show business. My favorite character I unearthed was a press agent named A. Toxin Worm (so help me) who did all kinds of crazy things in the late nineteenth century like spreading sawdust on the streets four blocks around Carnegie Hall so that the pianist Myra Hess wouldn't be disturbed by the sound of horse-drawn carriages as she rested in her Carnegie Hall apartment the night before she performed.

We decided to reconstruct the old-time publicity stunt in all its lunacy, and I sat many a night in Downey's, hatching plans to trick the New York media into mentioning the name of our pictures. There were seven daily newspapers in New York in those days, so there was a lot of space to fill.

We started slowly. The picture was *The Gallant Hours* with James Cagney as Admiral "Bull" Halsey in World War II. We opened at the Palace Theatre (which had flopped over to a straight movie policy in the late 1950s) and had navy signal flags run straight up from the top of the marquee to the top of the building. Sailors who could decode the flags would notice that they said "Screw the Navy!"

I waited. Nothing happened. Nobody noticed.

So I made the first of many phone calls that came to be my trademark. Posing as the indignant mother of a martyred American sailor, I raised my voice a full octave and called the Associated Press to tell them about the outrage at the Palace.

"How do you know?" asked the genuinely interested AP man.

"Because," I said, "I read flags! And they oughta be ashamed!"

They sent a man.

We indignantly denied that we had any knowledge of this "tasteless practical joke."

"Somebody's head will roll," my boss pronounced solemnly.

We made five of the seven papers. The *Journal-American* headlined the entertainment page "FOULMOUTH ON BROADWAY! HALSEY DEFAMED!" The *Times* declined.

Not long after that, we released a picture called *The Naked Maja*, starring Ava Gardner, a dreadful little movie about Francisco Goya's nude portrait of the duchess of Alba. The picture was terrible. Drastic measures were called for.

In those days there was a four-story-high billboard on the west side of Broadway extending from Forty-third to

Forty-fifth Street. It was the world's biggest sign, and we painted the duchess of Alba on it, stark naked and two blocks long. She materialized slowly, over a period of a couple of weeks, with the racier parts of her anatomy saved for last. Since the duchess had Ms. Gardner's face, the buzz on Broadway was understandable, and to keep the pot boiling we made a series of outraged calls to the papers as the representative of a half a dozen different religions. I even invented the Society for the Monitoring of Unwholesome Trash (SMUT), which sent several boxes of petitions to all the newspapers.

But the pièce de résistance was the curtain.

As the sign painters closed in on Alba-Gardner's most treasured area, we had a canvas curtain hung on a forty-foot wooden pole and lowered into place, obscuring the junction of the duchess's abdomen and legs. I reported sadly to anyone who would listen that we were bowing to the wishes of the religious community.

And then I called again, this time as a flaming liberal, chairman of the nonexistent Times Square ACLU. I was infuriated at the curtain, which I called "the most egregious attack on freedom of speech since the Inquisition."

By this time we had been in the papers for six days and I needed a change of pace, so we called an outdoor press conference at the sign announcing that we would lower the curtain. With the old 16-millimeter TV news cameras grinding and our usual army of hired photographers popping flashbulbs on empty cameras, the curtain descended, revealing the duchess wearing a pair of scarlet silk panties.

Our final gesture was a second press conference, held in the United Artists offices, in which we confessed every-thing—the phony phone calls, the fake SMUT petitions, everything. That kept the story alive for *another* two days.

And then there was *The Vikings.* I don't remember much about the movie, only Kirk Douglas, Tony Curtis, and Janet Leigh romping around in some very cold weather. The pic-ture needed a lot of help from our department, so we orga-nized one of our more elaborate publicity stunts.

During filming, a full-scale functional Viking ship had been built. So we hired some unemployed Norwegians to sail and row it across the Atlantic. They were supposed to follow the route of Leif Eriksson and arrive at a west side pier just in time for opening night.

Hiding a specially mounted inboard motor and two cases of Scotch, they took off for America in an elaborate ceremony held at the Norwegian port of Trondheim. As soon as they were out of sight, they broke out both the motor and the Scotch.

Needless to say, we had briefed the New York papers and provided a daily bulletin that included a map of the north Atlantic showing the progress of our intrepid sailors who turned out to be a scruffy, contentious lot who were lucky as hell to have perfect weather all the way across.

We were in radio contact twice daily so I knew that other than a few fistfights, everything had gone well enough for the first week. Then I woke up one morning and there was *nothing* in the New York papers, not a K head, not a col-umn item.

This was real trouble.

UA had made an enormous investment in this project, and the New York papers were bored already. We had run out of fake mid-Atlantic hurricanes, so I called up my pal Nick Clooney, the entertainment page editor of the *Journal-American*. It was early. I was sober.

"Mutiny," said Nick.

"What?"

"Have the crew mutiny, murder the captain, and head for Brazil."

I said, "How about, the crew mutinies, the captain heroically restores order, and they make New York in time for the opening with two men in chains?"

"Not bad," said Nick, "not bad."

I radioed the Viking ship, "SEND ME FOLLOW-ING MESSAGE: 'CREW MUTINIED, CAPTAIN WOUNDED, MORE LATER.' REYNOLDS, NEW YORK."

Nick Clooney was a genius; the tabloids went crazy. *The Vikings* grossed a half million in its first week, and that was back when it cost $1.50 to go to the movies.

There was lot of Damon Runyon's Broadway left by the time I got there. Right next door to Luigi's was Sammy's Ticket Agency, one of those joints where the tourists got taken for twice the price because they needed a Broadway seat that very night. Sammy needed a lot of runners, and that whole parade of Broadway characters, including the little guy with no legs on the dolly, the phony blind man, and the fat lady with a red wig, came by each night. Sammy would give them each two dollars to run tickets over to the tourist hotels.

Sammy had a top lieutenant named Monte, who was my favorite Broadway character, a beautiful man. A couple of years later, when I was in the civil rights movement, I was arrested on the steps of City Hall during a CORE demonstration, and a picture of me being carried off by a squad of New York cops filled the entire front page of the *Daily Mirror*.

Many years later, when I was down on my luck, Monte, who knew I was a hopeless drunk, pulled me out of the gutter on Forty-ninth Street one night, took me inside Sammy's, and showed me that front page of the *Mirror*, which he had framed and hung up in the middle of the show posters.

"Look, Beverly," said this nice guy, "you were the biggest man in town that day."

Broadway was like that then and always. When I had a few dollars, I could eat at the Russian Tea Room and talk to Al Hirschfeld. When I didn't, I could drink some wine with Nat Rubin, an old guy who made a meager living selling advertising space on the shirtbands of all the Chinese laundries in the neighborhood.

But to make the story come out even, I'll tell you about the night I stumbled into Anton LeBeaux—you remember, the guy who re-enlisted for a living.

He was playing the piano in one of the taxi dance halls next to the cigar store on Fiftieth Street. I was drunk and broke and wearing last year's underwear. Anton, who was also drunk but in a spotless full-dress uniform and sporting a new Good Conduct Medal, greeted me like a long-lost brother, stuffed a few dollars in my shirt pocket, and sat down at the piano.

He played me a song he had written that night. I remember the last line . . . I remember it like it was yesterday.

> *Give me a two-dollar bottle with a five-dollar smell,*
> *And I'll just walk my own sweet lonely way to hell.*

Paying My Dues

IT WAS LIKE this: Three white guys, two of them drunk, were riding around New York City in a 1950 Dodge in the fall of 1960. Happily, the driver was sober, and the two drunks were in the backseat barking orders as they studied a large road map of the city.

I barked first, "This is big! Twenty-six Woolworth stores and we got fifteen covered. George!" I leaned over and tapped the driver, "head for Forty-second and First. That's an NAACP picket line and they probably won't show up."

"To hell with the NAACP," slobbered Jack Barney, my buddy in the backseat who had a pint of Red Label in the vest pocket of his corduroy jacket. "I have," he announced, "decided on the anthem! New lyrics to 'Onward Christian Soldiers'!"

There was a two-beat pause before George stomped on the brakes. Jack and I pitched forward.

I cracked my head seriously on the driver's seat, and Jack dived all the way over the front passenger seat and landed upside down looking *up* at George, all pink and puckish and very drunk.

" 'Onward Christian Soldiers'?" said George Goldstein malevolently, " 'Onward *Christian* Soldiers'!"

"I forgot," said upside-down Jack to rightside-up George, "a lot of the Christian Soldiers will be Jewish."

This silly tableau in the middle of Manhattan traffic

was all my sister's fault. About a year before, I had called her from my desk at United Artists, where I had been stored in the publicity department by my ex-in-laws. Sissy (she'll never forgive me for using her childhood nickname in this story) was already a big-shot doctor in Washington, D.C., and I was getting a reputation in the family as a loser and a drunk who was circling my destiny over a back booth of Jim Downey's saloon on Eighth Ave.

On the phone I told my sister that I hated the movie business and wanted to do something useful with my life. She suggested that I call Marvin Rich at the National Office of CORE down on Park Row right across from City Hall.

You see, Sissy had paid her civil rights dues in the fifties as a leader of the Washington and Baltimore chapters of a tiny organization named the Congress of Racial Equality. CORE was eighteen years old in 1960, founded by James Farmer in Chicago in 1942 when he and some friends had sat down to eat at Jack Spratt's, a segregated restaurant. Farmer had made the intellectual link between the nonviolence of Mahatma Gandhi and the struggle for Negro freedom. CORE had bumped along for those eighteen years with a scattering of chapters on the East Coast, and although they had organized some brave and spirited protests, nobody much noticed or cared, with the notable exception of the prescient Eleanor Roosevelt.

I called Marvin, and he was delighted to recruit an uptown publicity type. For years, CORE people had been quietly getting their heads cracked open, sitting-in in segregated restaurants, and Marvin, like crafty old Gandhi himself, knew the value of some serious New York ink.

Marvin even made me a member of the National Action Council of CORE. Since they met during the daytime, I was able to attend meetings sober and actually make some constructive suggestions.

Sissy was right; it was fast becoming a heady, exciting period in America, and I had, through a combination of boredom and luck, landed in the right place at the right time.

What we now call the movement really busted loose in February of 1960 when a group of black divinity students sat down at a segregated Woolworth five-and-dime lunch counter in Greensboro, North Carolina. They were promptly arrested and thrown in jail. CORE got the word in New York and immediately sent one of our best field organizers, Gordon Carey, down to Greensboro to conduct workshops in nonviolence and try to spread the protest around the South to other Woolworth lunch counters. Woolworth was a godsend, a very visible national chain that was everybody's next-door neighbor, an American fixture that turned pocket change into pennywhistles and even had a scandalous heiress romping around the world marrying everybody in sight.

The Woolworth lunch counter sit-ins spread all over. Gordon had been busy.

Up in New York City we called for a national boycott of Woolworth stores everywhere in the nation. Marvin Rich, the steady hand on CORE's tiller, then made a mistake. He asked me to help organize the Woolworth picketing.

I immediately recruited my two smartest drinking buddies, Jack Barney and George Goldstein, and we bought a map of the five boroughs, a cork bulletin board, and some colored pushpins. We figured out where the Woolworth stores were and got on the phone, calling every organization we could think of to join us on picket lines throughout the city.

It must've been time. Everybody we called said yes.

And that was why three smart-assed white boys were running around New York City in a 1950 Dodge convinced we were God's gift to a fledgling civil rights movement that breathlessly awaited our decision on such matters as where to demonstrate, what to wear, and what to sing.

" 'The Battle Hymn of the Republic'!" squealed Jack. "New lyrics!"

"You're gonna improve on 'trampling out the vintage where the grapes of wrath are stored'?" asked George.

"And we oughta wear suits," I added. "Everybody wears a black suit with a black tie. Long black picket lines against the horizon," I saw the future, "with umbrellas!"

"Umbrellas!" shouted Jack, "that's our symbol! Great black umbrellas everywhere! Even on the stationery!"

"Not bad," agreed George. "I like the umbrellas, but the suits are out."

"What's wrong with the suits?" I asked.

"Too expensive," said George sternly, "and too hot in the South."

"Right," I said. "Forget the suits."

Despite the sophomoric, patronizing dialogue, it was, in the end, some serious business. After all, Jack Barney, George Goldstein, and, yes, even I, Beverly Reynolds, were there, in the early years of this nation's first healing since Reconstruction. We may have been fast-talkin' pompous little wiseguys from New York, but we *were there*, taking our turn in the American lists, trying to fix things that had been broken for five hundred years.

We had always been great talkers and had closed a lot of bars pontificating about the lot of our Negro brothers, but this time we were actually doing something about it. It was just too goddamn good to be true. We simply didn't know what to do with our good luck, so we drank whiskey, composed slogans, and walked in circles. Don't misunderstand me. We were little more than bit players, extras . . . but that was a good deal more than most folks.

As I look back, I can see that our principal problem was that we didn't know much about the people we had set out to save. Being black in America in 1960 was to have an ancestry of insult, a great accumulation of small and large grievances, a five-hundred-year pile of torn promises with the Emancipation Proclamation lying somewhere in the middle.

For example, when CORE's senior black field secretary, Sam Briscoe, got home from the Second World War, he started taking his neighbors down to the courthouse in

Sumter, South Carolina, to register to vote. He figured he'd earned it. They goddamn near lynched him.

So the three guys in the Dodge were something of an absurdity, a made-in-America absurdity. But it was a new beginning, and new beginnings required new tactics and all sorts of lunatics.

As we turned the corner at First Avenue and Forty-second Street, Jack Barney, author of "The Battle Hymn of the Republic" plan, suddenly said, "Everybody shut up and listen."

I was wrong. The NAACP picket line was enormous, running the entire length of the long red Woolworth sign. But the marchers were absolutely still, surrounding a tall young man with a big old twelve-string guitar. He had a cranky, aching voice that could break your heart. He was singing an old song on a new stage.

It was Pete Seeger, and for the first time in our lives we heard "We Shall Overcome."

SOMEWHERE THROUGH HERE, the three musketeers got our first lesson in humility when we met Bill Smoke. Attorney Smoke was a careless, noisy, wise, and funny black lawyer who liked himself so much that he was honestly astonished that racial discrimination existed at all.

Bill popped into the civil rights family without so much as a nod and immediately saw himself as man of policy who would reorganize the movement, parse the future, and generally straighten out this clutch of white boys who had fallen into to what was to be, in Bill's words, America's "redemption." He went to work on George, Jack, and me with a lot of such talk, and we were quickly and properly riddled with guilt. We actually moved our regular saloon from Louie's on Sheridan Square to Gar's Bar on Park Row to accommodate our new drinking partner who held forth with blood-soaked African-American history and ways to whack the common law into line.

If we were the musketeers, Bill was the king of France.

One thing about Bill Smoke, you didn't make jokes about his last name. To this day, I don't know if it was his real name, but Bill played it like a virtuoso, lying in wait for you to say something racial like "Smoky" so he could strafe you with something like, "You peckerwood son of a bitch! You wanna say 'nigger,' say 'nigger'! You Irish cracker! Be a man! Spit it out!"

After which I would pick up my pieces and leave the room.

By now it was getting to be the early winter of 1960 and, as you know, New York City doesn't work in the winter. Elevators panic, the subway ices up, and people generally lose touch with one another separated by fat coats and knit caps that cover your face.

The Woolworth picket lines dwindled as it got colder, and the three musketeers and the king of France zipped around town in the old Dodge trying to find ways to keep the things happening. We got the phone number of David Susskind, the father of the television talk show, and convinced him that a two-hour debate on civil rights was long overdue. The problem was that we couldn't find anybody to argue with us until Ralph Kilpatrick agreed to join the panel. In the end, he gave as good as he got from this covey of amateurs who had just been flushed out of Gar's Bar.

And there were terrible and wounding days to come. Over the next five years more than thirty civil rights workers would be killed and literally hundreds battered and beaten in the struggle. Hundreds of thousands of days would be spent in the prisons and county jails of the South, and grand and eloquent men like James Farmer would emerge from years of waiting to capture the day.

Even the booze diminished for a while. I remember a particularly sober and touching evening when the four of us visited the playwright Lorraine Hansberry, who was profoundly ill and talked to us from her bed. I don't remember everything she said, but her eyes burned through me when she talked of what she called the "unspeakable" history of the black American, and she asked each of us to embrace her briefly as she gave us her blessing and our fiercest challenge. She died untimely on the threshold.

We were much too busy to notice Christmas, but I distinctly remember carols coming out of Gar's jukebox when somebody rushed in and told us that Marvin Rich wanted to see Bill and me upstairs. The messenger added cryptically, "You're going south."

You see, the civil rights movement had not yet achieved its "Selma celebrity," so Marvin was short of troops and reduced to sending bozos like me on missions to the South.

We were chasing butterflies and one had landed on the Woolworth lunch counter in Lynchburg, Virginia. (Before I forget, Lynchburg was allegedly named after John Lynch, whose last name became a verb because his brother Charles loved to string up the neighbors. More recently, Jerry Falwell tastefully chose Lynchburg as the home of his ministry.)

Anyway, an almost saintly, disciplined group of black Baptist students had asked to be served at the Woolworth in Lynchburg, and the whole lot of them had been roughed up and tossed in jail. Their first court appearance was in two days and Marvin had made arrangements for Bill Smoke to be their lawyer. We had a policy that nobody traveled alone, so I was chosen to make the trip with Bill.

Now understand what we're talking about here. We're talking about a zany, certifiable black attorney and a permanently hung-over white wimp being sent into battle armed with only the moral brass of Mahatma Gandhi and what the Irish call a terrible thirst.

We took the train to Washington, D.C., that evening, rented a car, and headed west into Virginia in the middle of a moonless night.

I drove. After all, Bill was the king of France, and the king of France has a chauffeur, right?

I like to tell this story in four parts.

Our first stop was for gas, a rookie civil rights worker mistake for not topping off the tank in Washington. The gas station was a small stain of fluorescent light in the Virginia backwoods, and as we got closer I saw a lot of very tough-looking white guys in bib overalls squeezing beer cans and sitting on the hoods of two pickup trucks. The trucks had shotgun racks in the back windows.

Bill said, "Pull in," and like a lemming, I obeyed.

We both got out and Bill got a skull-faced young man to fill the tank. Now remember, this was 1960, and the sight of a black man and a white man, traveling together, dressed in city clothes, raised the local temperature ever so much. The white guys jumped down off the trucks and were headed slowly in our direction when Bill decided to raise the ante.

He kissed me.

That's right, a big, wet kiss right on the mouth.

The rednecks went crazy.

Somebody screamed "get 'em!" and a bent beer can bounced off my elbow as we jumped in the car and took off. The nozzle of the gas hose yanked out and we thundered down the two-lane cement highway trailing a stream of fuel. The chase was on as both pickup trucks pulled onto the road and roared after us. I floored the accelerator and prayed that we had rented a Maserati. For about five minutes it was like a bad movie, but we slowly pulled away from the pickup trucks, and eventually they gave up.

During this entire episode Bill was laughing so hard that I got confused and instead of yelling obscenities at him, I began to wonder if this was some sort of formal hazing ritual that I was supposed to go through as a civil rights newcomer in the South. I had no idea that the simple truth was that I was, for the moment, hanging out with a madman.

That's one.

Bill stole a gas cap in the next town. Thanks a lot, Bill.

We dawdled the next fifty miles or so and arrived in Hopewell, Virginia, where another demonstration had taken place, to file some papers when the courthouse opened at nine A.M. They were important papers, various motions, appropriate and even sometimes crucial in civil rights cases. As we rode into Hopewell, I noticed that Bill was erasing the names, dates, and signatures on the papers, and as soon as we came to a stop, he lettered in new names and dates and re-signed them with a different name.

I said, "Is that legal? Don't we have to be very careful down here? Don't they throw away the key for the slightest little thing?"

Bill Smoke smiled wearily and said, "These pecker-woods can't read."

Not reassured, I drove on to Lynchburg, and we pulled up in front of the Woolworth at about ten o'clock.

It was a thrilling, stirring scene. Maybe fifty young black men and women, dressed in blue and black college uniforms, were walking a slow circle in front of the store. Their absolute, disciplined silence at the center of a howling, livid mob of white Lynchburg citizens was magnificent. I saw for the first time what we had been talking about up in New York. There was a lucid, abiding strength in that picket line that would surely overcome any resistance that the South, with all its brutal history, could muster.

Bill and I joined the line. We grabbed cardboard placards and started circling. The crowd enclosing the picket line could easily spot an outsider, particularly a white one, and someone immediately spat on me and screamed, "Nigger lover!"

We went round and round, the temper of the crowd rising with each circuit. I saw Bill whispering to the student leaders. He walked over to me and said, "I'll be right back."

With that, everyone on our side disappeared. *Disappeared!* The students melted away, Bill melted away, and I was left alone in the middle of a mob. I looked down at the forlorn sign that had been looped around my neck, saying something heroic like FREEDOM NOW, and the crowd began to close in. I remember one particularly ugly, skinny old man who had his hand in his pocket as if he were fingering a knife or a gun. I was going to be goddamned if I was going to run, but I gotta tell you I was heart-attack scared. It lasted maybe five minutes, but I was sure an hour had passed before I heard the screech of a car and I cut through the mob to the curb to see my pal Bill roar up in our car, throw open the passenger door, and yell, "Jump in, hero!"

That's two.

By this time I was an emotional wreck. I had been up all night, kissed, deserted, and nearly killed, but William Smoke, Esquire, was having the time of his life. As we sped away down Main Street, he slapped me on the back and pronounced, "Well done!"

All I could do was sputter.

Now the reason we were in Lynchburg in the first place was to represent twenty-two young divinity students who had been jailed the week before and were due in court that morning. We drove directly to the courthouse and when we got inside, Bill put on his "serious advocate" look and asked me to sit next to him at the defense table. I was so disoriented by everything that I just sat down, suspecting nothing.

The twenty-two student defendants filed in respectfully and sat in two rows to our left. We were instructed to rise, and the judge came in, a wizened old specter who was probably the great-grandson of the city's namesake.

The judge banged his gavel, and Bill rose solemnly.

"Your honor," he said.

"Boy?" the judge answered.

"Your honor," Bill continued unperturbed, "I would like to introduce my distinguished colleague, the Honorable Beverly Reynolds, the assistant attorney general of the sovereign State of New York."

And he wasn't even smiling.

Here I was, in Lynchburg, Virginia, inside a heavily guarded courtroom, impersonating both a lawyer and a public official. If the judge had any idea I really was a quickly aging press agent, he probably would have hung me at sunrise.

But he didn't. He simply grumbled something about "Goddamn Yankees" and proceeded with the hearing. About a half hour later, with the hearing over and the kids sent back to jail for trying to eat lunch in a five-and-ten-cents store, we got the hell out of there. I was having severe breathing distress.

As soon as we were out of earshot of the courtroom,

I started screaming, "What the hell was that? Attorney god-damn general of what?!"

That's three.

Bill suggested we have a drink. Finally we agreed on something. Finally it was over. Little did I know.

We headed for a bar in the black section of town. It was the first story of a three-story frame house, and it sported an aluminum sign announcing "Bernie's."

Bill said, "You go on in while I park the car."

I was very thirsty when I stepped through the front door. I was home. I was safe.

But then the whole place, including the jukebox, came to a sudden, deathly stop.

Apparently no white man had entered that saloon since 1873. I saw about thirty very angry black men, fists clenched, ready to do me in. Just as the bartender was reaching for his baseball bat, Bill came in behind me and held up both hands for silence.

"This," said William Sonofabitch Smoke, "is Beverly Reynolds, the brave young white boy from New York City who walked the picket line alone this morning!"

A rousing cheer went up and I was lifted and seated on the bar itself and supplied with liquor and congratulations late on into the night.

It was one hell of a party. It turned out that every secretary and janitor, every black worker on Main Street across from Woolworth, had watched me walk the picket line that morning, and I was, as Bill had announced, something of a local hero for a day.

That is four.

We slept it off in somebody's house that night. As an old veteran of the southern wars, I flew out the next morning back to New York City to lord it over Jack and George.

Bill headed west and south, chasing the butterfly of freedom.

I never saw him again.

The Heart Attack

VICTOR AND I were a pair of eccentric old grouse, our women gone, the apartment a shambles. I was a drunk, and he was crazy. So when I had the heart attack, it was more like a punctuation mark than a catastrophe. You might even argue that the heart attack was a wonderful thing; it stopped me smoking and drinking for a while, and for a couple of days Victor didn't have to think or talk about his troubles.

I had had plenty of warnings. A week before the big night I stopped for dinner with my friend Evelyn at a place called Lucy's on Route 7 in Connecticut. During an excellent dinner I had some trouble catching my breath. It was a frightening experience because you actually hear your brain telling your lungs to breathe in one language and the lungs are listening in another. I stepped outside and drew in some country air and was, for the moment, all right. Evelyn demanded that I see a doctor, but I playacted brave and said it was nothing, although the truth is I was very frightened.

And then there was the spitting. For about a month, I was spitting all the time. Indoors and out I would spit on the rug or on the floor or on the grass. It even offended Victor, who shouldn't complain because the bowl of his pipe, which was never out of his hand, leaked saliva.

So there we were on the big night, in a ground-level duplex apartment dotted with spit stains. Victor was asleep upstairs in the small room with his dog, Hector (they both snored), and I had passed out on the downstairs couch after sucking up the last taste of Scotch in the neighborhood.

I woke up at about three A.M., fighting for each breath. As I remember it, there was no pain at all, just the terrible fear that I would not have enough air to finish the next breath. Something big was happening to Beverly Reynolds, who had sailed through life on a sea of whiskey and fried chicken certain that the world was round and the sea was endless.

With my head sort of cockeyed (I'd found a breathing position), I was able to throw off my dirty pink blanket and stand up. I called out to Victor upstairs who snuffled and grunted twice before waking up.

"I think I'm having a heart attack, Victor," I gasped on my next exhale. "Got a minute?"

There was a sudden silence in Victor's room and then a low "Oh my God." That was followed by the yelp of a dog being stepped on, which was followed in turn by stumbling sounds in the hallway, and then Victor fell down fourteen stairs. He landed at my feet in a great clatter, whimpering, "I think I broke something."

"Well," I said, "whatever it is, it'll mend. Would you mind getting me over to the emergency room at Beekman Downtown?"

Victor stood up and panicked. First, he ran out the front door and was standing in front of our neighbor's when he realized he was naked. Then he ran back into the apartment and zipped past me and up the stairs to find his pants.

By this time Hector was barking and I was beginning to think I was on my own.

The breathing was a little easier as I stuffed my wallet in my pants pocket (I had, as usual, gone to sleep fully dressed), and I walked out the front door and through the courtyard in a sort of trance. My head was like a balloon, and I was being blown along, making, I thought, long strides like a man walking on the moon. At the corner of Greenwich and Harrison streets a taxicab was idling. I jumped in and said, "The emergency room at Beekman Hospital. I think I'm having a heart attack."

The driver's head rotated, and I saw the uncomprehending face of an Azerbaijani. "Where's that?" he said with a thick Persian accent.

Victor, who had jumped in on the other side of the cab, sized up the situation and panicked again. "Whattayoumean 'where's that?' You're supposed to know where the hospitals are! Whattayoumean 'where's that?' "

"This is not helpful," I started, but Victor was completely crazy.

"We'll walk!" he announced, tugging at me. "If necessary, I'll carry you!"

"Shut the door, Victor," I said, exasperated. "Driver, take the next left and don't stop for red lights, I'M HAVING A HEART ATTACK!" My announcement was for everyone within hearing.

The cab broad-jumped forty feet and screamed a left turn on Jay Street. The driver pressed the horn, and we thundered through the dark downtown streets like the Twentieth Century Limited with me screaming "Left again! Right! No! Goddamn it, you missed the corner! Take a left! Two blocks. Now right!" And finally we were there. It was such an accomplishment that despite our momentary differences, I gave the driver a twenty-dollar bill.

Victor had jumped out and and got all the way up the ramp to the emergency entrance before he realized that he had left me behind in the cab.

"Where the hell are you?" Victor said pitifully. "You're having a heart attack!"

"Thanks, Victor," I answered as I fell up the ramp and through the glass doors.

The Emergency Room lobby at Beekman is a dark and mean place, darker and meaner than it has to be. A couple of rows of broken people sat in green plastic chairs waiting for their turn. But I have to admit that when I told the lady who looked like a donkey that I was having trouble breathing, she and an enormous guard put me right into a wheelchair and rolled me into one of those nooks with the frail, sliding curtains. I was lifted onto a vinyl-covered gurney and immediately plugged into an electrocardiograph, a daddy longlegs of a machine that was to become a sticky pal of mine for the foreseeable future.

Keep in mind that I was completely awake during the next couple of hours and my eyes and brain darted about looking for any evidence that I was going to die that night, that Beverly Reynolds was going to be snuffed after having written only four impudent plays.

The doctor who saved my life was a burly black

resident. After reading the electrocardiogram, he slapped a golf-ball-sized batch of what appeared to be brown Play-Doh onto my chest and handed me a couple of pills that gave me some immediate relief. This resident was also a sensitive doctor. When he first read the tape his expression didn't change and he didn't gasp, so I was of the opinion that I might live a little longer.

The problem, of course, was Victor.

Victor had trailed the wheelchair parade and was pacing back and forth on the other side of the curtain. I asked the doctor if there was a telephone handy and someone plugged one in right around the corner in the next nook. I asked Victor to call Evelyn and my sister, the doctor, in Washington. After a muffled argument about how to call long distance, Victor got Sissy on the phone, and she, in turn, talked to the resident at some professional length. After that conversation, which I couldn't hear, my sister talked to Victor.

The edge of my curtain had slid back so I was able to see and hear Victor on the telephone talking to Sissy. Victor's face was drained to pure white and he was slowly moving his head from left to right. "Bad as that," he said. "My God," he added, in case I had missed anything.

So this was it, I thought, I'm going to die, right here, right now. In front of everybody.

But I didn't. God had funnier plans.

Phantasmagoria is the word for the Cardiac Care Unit at Beekman Downtown Hospital. They wheeled me up there on the vinyl gurney hooked into an IV.

It was a movie. All over this dimly lit large room people were lying on gurneys, all scattered around in no particular order. In between the gurneys were more people wearing white gowns with words stenciled on their pockets. A great octopus was on the ceiling, with wires and tubes coming down from it hooked to the people on the gurneys.

But the damnedest thing was the sound. There was this low muttering that orchestrated bits of dialogue that sounded something like, "Mary? Mary! Can you hear me, Mary? Talk to me, Mary! Stay awake, Mary!"

I was lying there, fully conscious, thumbing through my life, and I suddenly realized that Mary was dead, and they rolled her out.

Then, from across the room, it was, "Max! Don't quit, Max! Talk to me, Max! Goddamn it, Max!" The doctor's voice stretched into a plea, "Please, Max, please . . . ," and his voice softened. I could hear real anguish in the doctor's voice.

Somewhere through here, a black apparition appeared at the bottom of my bed. I think it said, "May I help you, my son?" but the Puerto Rican accent was so thick that I probably got it wrong. But there was no mistaking his intentions when I focused and saw this chunky black-suited priest holding a huge rosary that tickled my feet.

"The rosary," I said lamely, and he immediately knelt down next to my gurney and started reciting the required prayers. I immediately did the math and figured out that I was in for fifty-three Hail Marys and six Our Fathers unless I made a move.

"No thank you, Father," I said, and this very nice man looked up at me pityingly, put his warm, caring hand on my forehead, and walked away in search of a proper Christian.

So this is the foxhole, I said to myself, and I'm an atheist.

Then I met Howie.

Howie is Dr. Howard Weintraub, a bantam rooster of a cardiologist who one night a week leaves his fancy spread up at the NYU Hospital to keep his hand in down at the Beekman CCU. Howie is the van Gogh of heart doctors. He attacks the problem of each patient with the broad brush of an impolite artist who is possessed by this strange and wonderful organ that sits in the middle of our chests.

Howie didn't bother to introduce himself, he just grabbed my chart and said, "You want me to be your doctor? There's some asshole on the phone who says he's your doctor. You want him on the phone or me in the flesh? It's up to you."

I meekly pointed at Howie. "You," I said, thinking that this little guy (the nametag on his lapel was level with my head) was a piece of work.

The doctor on the phone was a friend of Evelyn's who had been waked up and told to take over. Evelyn's doctor gratefully went back to sleep.

A word about Evelyn. Evelyn is a beautiful woman with whom I was in love and was also my personal therapist, squeeze, and scold. Her only known character weakness was me, and since she knew me better than anyone else knew me, I am fairly certain that when I called her at four in the morning from the curtain nook, she thought that I was drunk and on one of my telephone sprees, a subject that gets lots of air time in AA meetings. But Victor got on the phone and scared the hell out of her as well, so she swung into action and was, I understand, outside the door of CCU all night. Evelyn was to be my companion for the next three months, decoding the medical ciphers, handling the light traffic of visitors, and, as I will explain later, being a caregiver of extraordinary merit.

Well, Howie and I made it through the night in the Cardiac Care Unit. It was like a Stravinsky dream sequence, which I remember as a night of bubbling lungs, nitroglycerine patches, and loud whispers. There are no windows in the CCU at Beekman. I have learned that when it comes to death settings, like operating rooms and intensive care areas, the New York City building code, which has required a window in every room since the turn of the century, does not apply.

In the morning, Howie dispatched me to a "stage-two" semiprivate hospital room on another floor where I was to meet the first of a series of roommates—a marvelous array of broken New Yorkers, who, like me, had suddenly been plucked out of our particular self-indulgence and sent to bed.

Evelyn, who was my first visitor, managed a fairly convincing smile and introduced me to Roscoe, my roommate, a black actor who had collapsed in the middle of the third act of a bad Off-Broadway play. "It was the goddamn play," Roscoe insisted. "It's a goddamn wonder the whole audience isn't up here."

The very next day Howie instructed me to walk round and round the ward pushing my IV rig before me in a pointless exercise that was supposed to keep my parts working while my heart leveled off. After a while, Roscoe was allowed to join me in my circuits, and he turned out to be a saucy fellow who had made a life's work out of playing white people on stage, making audiences wince. Roscoe was running his own civil rights movement within the larger, more famous one. It was a subtle business, he eventually explained, in which he was pushing the liberal envelope with black Chekhov papas and even a soul-stricken Hamlet. Everybody hired him, not big time, mind you, but down in the boutique theater he was making a nice living.

Ever alert, I read all of this exercise stuff and other hospital signals such as virtually unlimited vistors and two new rooms on successively higher floors in two weeks as evidence that I was either doomed or was about to be discharged as cured.

If it was the latter, it meant I could head directly to the Beekman Bar, a saloon right up the street where I had once been flattened by a fireman for asking him what he was going to be when he grew up.

But this was not the case at all, Evelyn explained. I was to go home briefly, not touch liquor, and wait for my next course of treatment, an angiogram. I had had a heart attack, she explained, a massive myocardial infarction, and if I took a drink or smoked a cigarette, she would leave me in the nearest gutter to die.

I believed her. I spent the next three weeks sitting on

my living room couch, wrapped in the pink blanket, sober as a judge.

My sister the doctor had of course buzzed Howie Weintraub, found him excellent, and was shuttling back and forth from Washington to New York keeping an eye on things. This angiogram, for example, was to be performed at Howie's main ranch, NYU Hospital, where they have a wonderful but curious arrangement called "the co-op," a parallel hospital where patients go when awaiting operations or procedures like my angiogram. The co-op is sort of like a very clean hotel that permits conjugal visits. So when I was moved into the co-op and Evelyn walked in with my suitcase, I slid an arm around her waist and nibbled her neck.

"Don't even think about it!" Evelyn announced, but I didn't believe her.

We made some wonderful love that morning. It was dangerous and glorious, sort of like screwing on Interstate 80.

After, Evelyn may have been furious, but she was smiling as she scolded me.

"What if your heart had popped again?" she asked after the fact. "You'd be dead."

"And in heaven," I said.

You can always tell how much real trouble you're in by the number of consent forms. The next morning, just before the angiogram, a lovely nurse showed up with a clipboardful.

They had me, literally (see below), by the balls. Some

doctor had said, "Oh, don't worry. We lose only two or three a year during the angiogram. It's no sweat at all." I felt completely vulnerable, but I had to go through with it. It was something like First Communion.

They rolled me over to the next building, stuck a probe in a vein that starts in my crotch, and turned on their television monitor. I was on full alert again, listening to every word spoken so I could figure out whether I was going to live or die. This procedure sends this probe all the way from your crotch to your heart, and by watching its progress through the veins around your heart on TV, they can tell how much Kentucky fried chicken is plugging up the flow of blood to your heart, which, in a crude sort of way, explains why some people have heart attacks.

There was a lot of "Oh, shit, that one's ninety percent full" and "See there, Beverly?"—everybody at NYU Hospital gets on a first-name basis immediately—"See that? We're gonna have to rewire. But don't worry, it's a piece of cake."

Some piece of cake, I thought, when the head nurse couldn't get my blood to clot at the entry wound and Howie had to be summoned to save the day.

When the full returns from the angiogram were in, it was clear that I was a perfect candidate for big-time bypass surgery. It seems that everybody was relieved. Terrific.

Now all this happened in 1982, when bypass surgery was in its adolescence. Nowadays it's pretty commonplace and even considered unnecessary if you qualify for alternatives such as angioplasty, a procedure like the angiogram in which a little collapsed balloon is sent through that vein and inflated when it reaches a blocked artery near the heart. But if you know anybody who has had the full bypass surgery, be nice. I'll give you a short description.

After you're under in another room with no windows, they take a power saw and cut your sternum (your chest bone) right up the middle. Then they open up your chest like French doors, reach in, and grab your heart. They hook you up to a heart-lung machine, which pumps and breathes for you, "bypassing" those two organs. Your heart, now emptied of your blood, turns white, and while they've got the sucker quiet, they cut out the old blocked veins and replace them with veins usually from the inside of your thigh. So you end up looking like the Confederate flag, with stripes down both legs and all over your chest. It also hurts. A lot.

After the angiogram, I was sent home to wait for my turn with the heart surgeon, Dr. O. Wayne Isom. My sister and I made this bloodcurdling decision to postpone the surgery until we could get Isom because he was supposed to be the best. You know the American drill, "Well," said Mrs. Proverbial from Kansas City, "we want the *top* man, from Vienna if possible." We've all seen too many movies.

Looking back, it's still a complicated call. I was, according to Howie, at serious risk for another heart attack, which would undoubtedly be fatal, so the operation should take place as soon as possible.

On the other hand, we now know that Dr. Isom probably saved my life. It turns out I've got this genetic oddity. One of my arteries runs *through* my heart instead of around it like everybody else's. I should have figured something might have been screwed up, since both of my small toes point the wrong way. The gist of it is, according to the legend I've been spreading ever since, no surgeon in the world had ever seen this through-the-heart deal except O. Wayne Isom, and even he had seen it only a few times. I don't know what the score is, but I made it, thanks to O. Wayne.

So Evelyn and I treaded water for a while. My sister found out about our shenanigans in the co-op before the angiogram and she declared a moratorium on sex. Victor with the dripping pipe was very solicitous, and Hector the dog, who didn't like me very much, was upset because I was home all day.

Finally, after a month of fake chest pains and explicit nightmares, the phone rang and O. Wayne gave me a date.

It was a beautiful October day when I checked into the main hospital; no co-op, no hanky-panky this time. I remember the weather because it occurred to me that when I went indoors it might be the last time I'd see the outdoors. I had the vivid image of going into a hole or a cave of some sort with enormous doors closing and locking behind me.

The operation had something like a 98 percent survival rate (the artery-through-the-heart anomaly hadn't yet shown up on the X rays), so I was fairly calm. I did notice that Evelyn and my sister were just a tad oversolicitous, sort of choosing their words carefully as one would write an elegy.

Up in the ready room, Dr. Isom came by and in a single sentence, "Don't worry, I'll fix you up," put my over-active imagination at rest.

One of the more tasteless events of that day was the efficient-looking young woman who arrived with a black briefcase to give me an intelligence test. You heard me right, intelligence test. She explained that they were doing "before" and "after" tests with this particular kind of surgery. The obvious question they were trying to answer was, When they stop your heart do you turn stupid? It was not exactly what I wanted to think about that afternoon, but I took the test because you generally do what you're told in large buildings with a lot of bedrooms.

That night they gave me some pills and shaved all the hair off me, *all* of it, and painted me yellow. So there I was, a sort of banana, alone in my room, waiting for my five A.M. appointment in another room with no windows.

Actually, I didn't see the woman right away when she came in, but just after the shaver left, I began to hear some soulful humming that I thought was an auditory side effect of the tranquilizer pills I had just taken. But pretty soon the humming became full-scale gospel singing, and I turned my head far enough to see an enormous black woman with a mop belting out "We Will Gather by the River" in a voice that rattled the venetian blinds. I didn't know what the hell to do. In my salad years, the sixties, I had heard a powerful lot of black church music, mostly at funeral services. Since I was the only other person in the room, it was obviously my soul that was being attended to, and I was goddamned if I wanted to be sung over like a mahogany coffin. Dr. Isom had promised to "fix me up," and that was the scenario I preferred. So I politely waited until she had finished a full verse and then asked her to stop, my exact words being, "Madam, this is my death and I'd like to pick the music." It was a mean thing to do, but then I never claimed I was a class act in a foxhole.

The last person I saw before the operation was my ubiquitous sister who, despite her professional standing as one of the nation's great neurologists, cried as she left the room.

By this time, with a weeping sister and gospel music, I was losing my hold on my doctor's optimism.

But I was getting dopier by the minute, so it didn't make a hell of a lot of difference. I do remember the trip on the rolling stretcher through the hallways and down the elevator (you know the movie shot). I even remember being rolled into the operating room and being lifted onto the table.

Then they did it (see above).

I woke up floating in a sweet pond of morphine. Boy, did I feel good. I called all the nurses over to my gurney and solemnly announced that I was going to give them the real skinny on Florence Nightingale. From Charing Cross to the Charge of the Light Brigade, I followed Florence across the face of Europe and into the muddy, unsanitary tents of the British army in the Crimean War.

Dr. Isom interrupted my lecture to announce that the

operation had been a complete success. "We had some complications," he added, "but you're going to be just fine."

It was at the word "complications" that I began to hurt. I am talking about *hurt.* As the morphine wore off, cowardice took its place, and I let everyone know about it. My head hurt, and my chest (with the recently closed French doors) was an agony. Even my ass hurt. In a few hours nothing worked except my mouth, which was begging for painkillers, enemas, throat lozenges, and any other analgesic up to and including a .38-caliber revolver with which I would have happily shot myself.

Finally, after three enemas and forty-four Percodans, I began to feel better.

And a week later, I was almost normal. The same efficient lady with the briefcase showed up, and I took another intelligence test. It had been my plan to fail deliberately because of their scientific insolence, but I couldn't do it. I passed with flying colors. Apparently the operation had made me smarter.

Finally, Evelyn took me home. I had scar instructions, eat instructions, and exercise instructions. I also had Victor.

He stood at the door of the apartment as Evelyn guided me across the flagstone plaza. Hector bounded over and dribbled on me. Victor handed me a huge drink of Scotch.

Everything was normal.

I was home.

I had learned nothing.

On the Harmfulness of Alcohol*

(You may want to pass this one up. It's short and it starts easily enough, but it gets ugly as it goes along. Be warned.)

*With apologies to Anton Chekhov.

THERE WAS THIS one cop for whom the word "brass" had been invented. He was a New York City police officer with a vengeance. He must have been a general or something because he had gold buttons and silver stars all over him. I even remember an antenna rising out of his hat, but then I was drunk and I might be mistaken.

In any case, he took one look at me and said, "Reynolds, your fly is open."

That wouldn't have been so bad; one can always turn to the wall and zip up one's fly. But I had just held a TV press conference and my open fly was on its way downtown in a can of videotape to make the morning news.

But I'm getting ahead of myself. I'm writing this little essay because it seems only fair that I explain how I survived my own thirst, indeed how it is possible that I am writing these tales at all after thirty-nine years of very dry martinis with a lemon peel, how I sobered up.

Now, in the fellowship, you don't *ever* claim you're cured. I honestly believe that alcoholism is an incurable disease and that I caught it from a string of great-aunts and great-uncles on my mother's side whose DNA was pickled in Ireland on one of those bitter cold islands where we hid from the Vikings in the ninth century.

I must hurry to add that my mom was a teetotaler, and

my father, aside from the occasional Wednesday night beer and poker, was as steady as she goes.

But I, as my Mom would have said, "took the cake." From that first sip of beer at the cast party following *The Glass Menagerie* in 1948 until February 16, 1986 (the night of the open fly), I drank an ocean of booze, pillaged and burned the countryside, talked a Bible of bullshit, applauded the guilty, and deflowered the innocent.

Otherwise, I was terrific.

If you hold this book up close to your nose, you will faintly smell the whiskey that I used to consume and you should feel no pity. Alcohol was my clipper ship that sailed me past all my problems, leaving chaos, broken promises, and wounded friends in its wake.

It's no joke. It damn near killed me, and through me it maimed a lot of otherwise excellent people. Forgive me.

So that brings me to that night with the cop and the press conference. That night became the morning that I quit.

It was like this.

In February of 1986 I was the director of public information for the New York City Housing Authority, an enormous agency that administers the local public housing program. It is my theory that most drunks who want to be writers end up as press agents, a squalid profession that permits us to write two-paragraph press releases instead of hundred-thousand-word novels. And worse, most press agents find themselves selling things they detest. But I was lucky; I was the spokesman for a noble program that put warm homes around poor people. Best of all it was a job I could handle between drinks with a smart mouth and a steel liver.

I was on duty twenty-four hours a day, which meant that all night long I received phone calls, usually calls about murder, mayhem, and broken boilers. It was my job to put a positive spin on the stories, but since I was routinely drunk when the calls came in, I usually blurted out the truth and developed an uncanny reputation with the local police reporters as a reliable and candid source.

Once in a long while one of our cops would be shot, a four-alarm crisis that would require me to call all my bosses, travel to the hospital, and handle the mob of press people who show up at bloodlettings.

Get the picture?

I had been drinking since noon on February 16 at my favorite saloon, Donahue's, on Murray Street. By six in the evening I was so drunk that Ben the bartender had confiscated my car keys and I stumbled home and fell asleep on the living room couch. I woke up a couple of times to suck on a Scotch bottle so when the phone rang at midnight, I was, using the most unpleasant synonym for very drunk, shit-faced.

A cop was down. A cop was dead. Deep in the forest of Brownsville projects, a brave Housing Authority police officer had been killed.

And the man principally responsible for telling his story to the world, the man who was paid handsomely to report those last few seconds of that young man's life with taste and unflagging dignity, was crocked.

I got dressed in a hurry, and a young woman police officer driving a radio car picked me up on the corner outside my house. I gave her an earful of stupid drunken homilies as she put on the siren and we careered through red lights and past a lot of barking dogs all the way to a hospital in the far reaches of Brooklyn.

Can you imagine her feelings on that trip? A brother officer who easily could have been she was shot to death, and she was riding to the scene with a flannel-mouthed big shot who reeked of twelve hours of booze coming out of his sweat glands.

We drove into a whomp of red lights and TV cameramen who mobbed me, but Saint Joan, my driver, put her arm around me and hustled me past the mob into the Emergency Room. I was the first civilian official of the Housing Authority to arrive, so there was nobody to say, "Get that drunk the hell outa here," and I proceeded on my cross-eyed way to interrupt a briefing being held for the top cops with "Wait a minute, give me that again" as I patted my pockets for a piece of paper and a pen.

I still have the notes I made that night. They are written around the edges of a Xerox of the Donahue's hockey pool and are indecipherable.

With a passing glance at the mother of the dead police officer who was doubled over with grief, I proceeded to hold a press conference. I got a gift from the god that watches over little children and drunks when a friend of mine, a very large deputy chief named Joseph Flanagan, sized up the situation and stood next to me in the flood of lights with his left hand gripping my right elbow in such a way that every time I opened my mouth he squeezed my elbow hard enough to snap it off. So he did all the talking at the press conference, and if the open fly is discounted, things were not all that bad so far.

Usually, the mayor and the police commissioner drop whatever they're doing and rush to the scene when a cop is down. But another major catastrophe involving the near-fatal burning of two firemen on the fourth floor of a Yorkville building had occurred a little earlier that same night, so the mayor and the commissioner never made it to our Brooklyn hospital.

Drunks love trouble. We zero in and obsess on a grievance with the speed of light.

That night I decided to be shocked and outraged at the fact that the mayor and the PC didn't come. Never mind the fire in Yorkville, never mind the two firemen fighting for their lives, I started collaring anybody handy and shouting, within earshot of the the press guys, that the mayor was a horse's ass and the police commissioner was a disgrace to his office because they wouldn't show up at the deathbed of a housing cop.

Maybe ten guys jumped me to shut me up, and after the big cop with the buttons and stars had allowed as how my fly was open, I was given back to Saint Joan, who drove me home and flushed me out of her car like a wet walrus onto my flagstone terrace. She sprayed Lysol where I'd been.

But that wasn't the end.

I woke up pie-eyed after a couple hours of sleep and took a mouthful of Scotch for breakfast in an effort to forget what had happened the night before. I weaved my way to work and headed straight for the office of Bill McDaniel who I knew had a jug in his desk. (Drunks know these things, like a guy on his way back from the South Pole knows where his next cache is.) I had saved Bill for just such an emergency, and he immediately poured me a waterglass full of whiskey, which I swallowed whole.

Then I went up to my own office, picked up the phone, and proceeded to call the police commissioner's press assistant. I knew the PC; he had once been chief of the Housing Police and we'd gone round and round a few times and even had a grudging admiration for each other.

Innocently, she took my call.

I started bellowing, calling the PC a lousy cop and an all-around son of a bitch for not coming to the hospital the night before. Of course I don't really remember everything I said, but I do remember the sound of her hanging up. It was the sound of a coffin closing.

I needed a drink.

But Donahue's was closed. I was astonished to discover that bars generally aren't open at nine-thirty A.M., so I went back home and passed out under the grand piano in my living room.

All hell broke loose back at the office. The PC called

my chairman who called my friend Roy who came over to my house and shook me awake. I was sound asleep in a puddle of piss under the piano.

My friend Roy is a great great man whom I will have much more to say about some day, but that morning the best he or anybody could do was to roll me out of my stinking little crib and put me to bed. He had been covering for me for years, but this time I had smashed everything in sight, used up every ounce of good will I had coming, and should have been taken out and shot without a blindfold.

But that's not what happens to drunks like me. I was given another, my ten thousandth, chance. And this time when I walked into an AA meeting I knew everybody in the room. I don't mean that I actually *knew* them, but I knew I was with my brothers and sisters because I knew the fear in their eyes and the size of their thirst.

You see, all we do is tell each other our stories and seek a kind of candor and harmony that keeps us from picking up a drink each new day.

In a way, we've just had a meeting, you and I, so I mustn't forget to tell you the most important thing.

It never ends. Ten years have passed and I still need that drink.

Intermission

RECOVERING DRUNKS ARE not perfect. Sometimes we think that the world is all fixed up because we are, for the moment, sober. We even showboat from time to time. Oh, I don't mean that we march into our old saloons and suck on a Diet Sprite in front of everybody. I mean that we have some secret places where we go and whisper, "Look here, God, I'm sober!" and a lovely peace descends on us.

The place I go is the park that fills up the huge block just below City Hall. A lot of my life has surrounded that park. On one side is the Housing Authority, and on the other is a redbrick building with turrets on top, the old national CORE office where we banged the world around in the sixties. Today, the old office is sealed off on the park side, as if some terrible political infection were lurking there.

One afternoon, soon after I had stopped drinking, I discovered that someone had planted a thirty-foot-by-ninety-foot American flag made out of red, white, and blue tulips in the middle of the park as if trying to exorcise the ghosts of the pacifists and troublemakers who once flourished across the street in the red castle.

I had just left an AA meeting and was feeling pretty proud of myself, giggling at the funny flag and bragging to God, when someone said out loud, "How about it, brother, got a dollar?"

And I turned and I looked and there was a black

woman with her hair like the burst of a black star and she was all bundled up in a khaki blanket sitting on a park bench next to a grizzled old white rummy, his hand embracing a pint of wine.

And I was just a little frightened, fishing out a dollar bill.

She said, "Thank you," as I turned away, trying to erase the picture.

But she had seen my eyes.

"Don't forget me," she said, "My name is Marigold."

My Name Is
Marigold

IT WAS CHRISTMAS Eve and Marigold decided that she was going to fix up the world. It was not an idle notion. She was determined to end nuclear proliferation, settle border disputes, feed everyone who needed to eat, and, since "Oh Little Town of Bethlehem" was her favorite Christmas carol, settle all accounts in the Middle East.

She told Thunder about her plan and at first he just laughed, took another swallow of warm wine from the bottle he kept between his belt and his stomach, slapped Marigold on the back, and said, "Well, hell, Marigold, how're you gonna do all that lookin' the way you do, your hair all stringy and full of rubber bands. Who's gonna listen when you go on in there lookin' like the Witch of West Broadway?"

It was true, Marigold's hair did look terrible. This was especially noticeable because Marigold and Thunder had spent that December on their grate outside a beauty parlor that had big pictures in the window of young women with wonderful clean hair all fixed up and combed around their heads.

After Thunder had made his speech, Marigold was scared to look at the pictures, but she bravely turned her head and about ten inches from her nose was the photograph of a young, perfectly ornamented black woman who could have gone anywhere and done anything.

For the first time that day, Marigold cried.

But putting the problem of her hair aside, there was the larger question of Marigold's credentials, her competence to handle international matters. Her qualifications were excellent: Marigold had spent the last eleven years on the streets of New York or in its jails or shelter system, and she had a powerful understanding of all sorts of people. Marigold knew, for example, when the pace of people walking along West Broadway had changed, when they began jerking their left arms upward to look at their watches, an awkward wooden soldier–like gesture that they all seemed to do at the same time, making the stream of once-generous office people into a silly stiff ballet. Needless to say, these new dancers, these hurrying people, filled up with themselves, now seldom tossed a coin into Thunder's hat, which led Marigold to the understandable conclusion that the people of the world had grown careless of one another.

And beyond these sweeping insights, she had much more specific gifts as a negotiator. Marigold was a legend in the tank on Centre Street where all the prisoners waiting to see the judge are collected in a large square cell with bars on all four sides. Because she was tall and fat and black and topped by a great smoky tangled head of hair, she was considered royalty. Even the most raucous of the drunks hitched up their pants and turned silent when Marigold held her own court, settling, over the years, hundreds of small disputes that the regular judges disdained, questions such as who worked which corner or whose turn it was to get the unbroken iron cots at the Baxter Street Shelter. Needless to say, she was very fair and remembered everyone's name and story without keeping notes. She was so fair, in fact, that when she was on the street there was often a line of petitioners leading up to her grate on West Broadway. Thunder, when he was able, kept the line orderly and quiet.

Marigold was black and Thunder was white, a matter of complete indifference to everyone.

At the moment, on the afternoon of Christmas Eve, the question of her hair was more important than anything else. The obvious answer was to pool some money from some of her friends and simply go into the beauty parlor and let them ply their trade. The problem with that plan was that the beauty parlor was owned and operated by the hurrying people who hated Marigold and Thunder and had called the police at least thirty times to have them removed from the grate in front of their store. In truth, Marigold didn't mind the police sweeps at all; in fact, they always seemed to come at the moment when she and Thunder were getting so cold that the square cell at Centre Street or the shelter was a welcome change.

Marigold considered the problem in her judicious way and got a wonderful idea, which she whispered to Thunder.

First, she knocked on the window of the beauty parlor, and a particularly unhappy lady (who looked nothing like the cardboard pictures) turned her head from the batch of hair that she was spraying and shook her finger at Marigold. While everyone was watching Marigold, Thunder opened the glass front door and stepped inside. At first, there was a great commotion as all the customers in various stages of repair, some with their heads stuck in aluminum rockets and others licking their fingers as they passed through the advertising pages of *Vanity Fair*, turned awkwardly, stretching their paper dusters, to look at Thunder. When he had their attention, and the room was silent, Thunder said, "Marigold wants to make a deal!"

And the deal was this. In return for a shampoo, comb-out, blow-dry, and mountainous set, Marigold and Thunder solemnly agreed immediately to move their home no less than two full blocks away to another grate. The fact was that Marigold had had her eye on that other grate ever since its regular tenant, Willie with the missing foot, had died. And since she fancied herself something of a "natural communist," she had trained herself not to get attached to property, so leaving the beauty parlor grate behind was not a painful loss.

When she first walked in, the beauty parlor people put Marigold in a chair in the back of the store and tried to draw a curtain to shut off the view of Marigold's hairdo from the street. But Marigold would have none of that because Thunder was selling spaces at the window to their friends and had squeezed thirteen scruffy street people across the two plate-glass windows and the plate-glass door at twenty cents a head.

So Marigold had an unpleasant fit and was moved to something of a throne, the chair nearest the window where her subjects could see her plainly. It was beginning to be a wonderful Christmas Eve. Marigold insisted on their biggest paper duster, a pink one that flowed all over her, sweeping over the arms of the chair almost all the way to the floor like a royal robe. And the beauty parlor people began to catch the spirit.

Her friends in the window were very impressed because *they* knew that Marigold was royalty, but it had never occurred to them that the regular people knew it too.

And, of course, gradually the word spread along West Broadway and onto Chambers and Murray streets, and the crowd around the beauty shop began to blossom. The Salvation Army marched its very small brass band all the way down from Broadway, bringing along, of course, the tripod and money pot. And much to Marigold's delight (she could hear the music through the window), they played "Oh Little Town of Bethlehem" and right there, in the middle of all that ceremony. Marigold cried for the second time that day.

From high in the air, maybe from the fiftieth floor of the World Trade Center, you could see that something marvelous was happening. The crowd around the beauty parlor spilled out into the street and, miraculously, all of the Christmas decorations everywhere in the offices, including the MERRY CHRISTMAS and HAPPY HOLIDAY letters strung together on the off-white walls and room dividers and the green plastic tinsel and the white foam messages sprayed on windows all around, these little tacky gestures seemed for the first time to be generous and tasteful acts of kindness and proper celebration.

Needless to say, the people working inside the beauty parlor soon forgot their fear of the poor people bearing down on their front window and warmed to their task. Even the unhappy lady smiled when the music began, and she personally took charge of Marigold's daunting head of hair.

The process took one and a half hours, just long enough to sustain the sentimental spirit of the crowd but not so long that the crowd around the beauty shop became unruly as the wine began to rise to the centers of the brain where wickedness begins. (Twenty free half-pints, believe it or not, were handed out by Pete, the owner of Savannah Liquors, who, like everyone else on the block, had gone a little balmy.) So as each stage of the transformation was completed—the shampoo and comb-out, the styling gels, and the triumphant set—the hair ascended, level by level with racks and rats administered by a circle of beauticians armed with combs and spray cans who glided around Marigold in an awkward dance, sculpting up and up until their arms would fail them. From time to time Marigold would turn to her audience in the window and nod her head or raise her hand slightly from the arm of the chair, much as Queen Victoria had indicated her approval to Lord Salisbury who had just suggested that the Boer War begin.

When the job was finished she thanked the beauty parlor people with a round of embraces and asked them if she could keep the pink duster as a memento. They folded it up carefully and she packed it in the ample pocket of her greatcoat. Thunder held out his arm, Pete of the liquor store opened the door, and Marigold and Thunder walked out into the crowd. She took measured steps, and at first there was silence, followed by a great roar of approval and applause that could be heard as far away as Warren Street. Marigold raised her hand again to signal silence, and when the crowd was quiet once again, she began to speak.

"Merry Christmas," said Marigold.

"Merry Christmas!" everyone shouted back.

"I got my hair done," she added unnecessarily, because the top of her head could be seen for blocks, a towering festoon of waves and wiggles, a virtual Christmas tree of hair atop Marigold who was already the tallest person in the neighborhood. "For free!" she added, and the crowd bellowed its approval even louder and turned toward the beauty parlor where the workers and customers had lined up across the inside of the window, smiling and waving. The street people applauded toward the window and the beauty parlor people bowed and curtsied in reply.

Marigold began again, "You all know Thunder, don't you now?"

Everyone knew Thunder.

"Well," she said, pausing for effect, "now that my hair is right, Thunder and me are gonna go uptown!"

It was a big surprise. Marigold at some time or another had touched almost everyone's life, and the way she said "Thunder and me are gonna go uptown" sounded pretty permanent, like they were leaving forever. The people on the street were shocked.

Before Marigold could explain, some shouted, "No!" and "Don't go, Marigold!" Others felt really sad, and there were even a few, the criminal element, who secretly thought With Marigold out of here, I can sleep anywhere and steal cans from anybody. But mostly, during that moment, people grumbled and felt sad.

"We're comin' right back," explained Marigold quickly. "We're gonna be gone just long enough so I can make a speech at the United Nations."

Well, *that* was different, and to most folks it made perfect sense. Of all the people in all the countries everywhere on earth, the folks in the crowd on West Broadway that day knew that Marigold was the world's very best diplomat and speaker and that she would make them very proud. The only thing they wondered was how she and Thunder had made the deal to speak at such a fancy place, but then they thought about the beauty parlor and how Marigold had got her hair done, and they figured she could do most anything at all.

What happened next was quite wonderful, even for a Christmas Eve.

The "Professor," a sad old drunk who had taught ethical conduct and logic at Princeton when he was younger, knew exactly where the United Nations was and how to get there, so he started the parade to the Lexington Avenue subway stop by lining up the Salvation Army brass band and leading it to the corner of West Broadway and Chambers Street, conducting with a long brass curtain rod that was handy. Someone found a broken aluminum kitchen chair with a yellow seat and Marigold sat down with great dignity and was, in turn, lifted high in the air, just behind the brass band, facing backward toward the crowd, which soon was transformed into a ragged column that began its journey of three long blocks to the subway station. Thunder held the two front legs of Marigold's chair up in the air. The only problem was that the Salvation Army band knew only Christmas carols and "Nearer My God to Thee," which were not marching music, so that the Professor's downbeat and the music were all confused in a merry Christmas way.

And so the dissonant and shabby and loud parade wound its way up the sidewalk on the north side of Chambers Street with the Professor at the front, the brass band caroling away, Marigold tipping this way and that in her sedan chair, and the scraggly pack of folks behind. After passing Church Street, Thunder realized that he had over-estimated his arm strength and, badly needing a drink from the bottle in his belt, let the chair down slowly. Marigold, who had nearly fallen off a half a dozen times, gratefully descended and began to walk, arm in arm with Thunder, who had been able to pull a mouthful of sweet enthusiasm from his bottle just in time.

Boldly, the Professor led the parade catercorner across the intersection at Broadway and Chambers Street, where the two traffic Brownies immediately understood the importance of the occasion and blew their whistles to hold the cars back. (It must be said that not a few of the paraders, far back in the line of march, made questionable gestures and shouted impolitely as they passed the lines of cars that had been abruptly stopped.)

The parade went on beside the Tweed Building, past the Surrogate's Court across the street, and made its way up onto the concrete plaza that surrounded the old green and ornate entrances to the Brooklyn Bridge station on the Lexington Avenue IRT. Here the Professor stopped and the Salvation Army brass band settled itself in its usual circle with the tripod and money pot in the middle and for some reason suddenly remembered how to play "Onward Christian Soldiers," which *was* a marching song, now played in concert rather than during the march when it could have helped to keep things in step and organized.

Thunder, meanwhile, had gone down the steps of the station entrance and pushed a handful of coins through the slot of the token booth and got two tokens in return. Actually, Thunder had collected more than ten dollars at the beauty parlor window by limiting each spectator to a half an hour and then reselling the spot at a higher price as the demand increased. Although he had more than enough money for four tokens (which would be needed for a round-trip), Thunder, as was his practice, kept the extra money in his pocket. It had been his experience that he might very well need the money and liquor store owners generally didn't like to sell their wine for subway tokens even though they were as good as gold.

As "Onward Christian Soldiers" ended, Thunder bounded up the steps of the station entrance and solemnly presented the two subway tokens to Marigold. There was another round of applause, and Marigold raised her hand slightly once again.

"We're gonna go now, Thunder and me, and we'll be back tonight, I promise. I want to thank you for the parade and . . . everything."

And at that moment, Marigold cried for the third time that day, and then, with Thunder close behind, hurried down the stairs. The last words they heard from the crowd was the tenor voice of the Professor shouting, "Take the number five to Forty-second Street!"

It had been a very long time since Marigold and Thunder had left the neighborhood. They lived conveniently close to all the Manhattan courthouses and when they were indisposed, they were transported no more than five or six blocks away from their grate in front of the beauty parlor. So it was a big, important deal when they were suddenly alone, without their friends, down in the subway station, clinging to each other and being stared at.

And they were a sight to see: Thunder in the suit he called his "street pajamas" and Marigold with her fountain of new hair atop the gold-trimmed black greatcoat she had found a week before in front of the sandwich shop.

Thunder fumbled them through the new turnstiles and they were watched by a transit cop who took notes because he was writing a book. It took all of their courage to climb aboard the number five express train when it finally arrived. Luckily, the two seats just to the right of the door were empty and they sat together, holding hands, all the way to Forty-second Street.

Before, sitting in the beauty parlor chair, Marigold had done some planning, not about what she was going to say when she addressed the United Nations, but about how she and Thunder were going to get into the assembly chamber and up to the microphone. Marigold was, after all, something of an expert on police and guards and things like that and was sure that she and Thunder could outwit the security system of the United Nations.

"They're not even New York City cops," she said to Thunder as they got out of the train at Forty-second Street."

"Who's not?" asked Thunder.

"Those guards at the United Nations," said Marigold as she adjusted her hair in the little mirror above the gum machine. "They're not real cops."

She turned to Thunder. "Buy a broom."

"Buy a what?"

"A broom," Marigold repeated. "And don't tell me you haven't got the money. I saw you sell those places at the window plain as day."

"A broom?" said Thunder.

"A broom," said Marigold and walked on up the steps, past Grand Central Station, and onto the street, trailing Christmas carol music that came from the loudspeakers in the huge waiting room and followed her into the open air.

Thunder *stole* a fine broom, a push broom with long black bristles, hardly used. He snatched it from a janitor's closet off a Grand Central tunnel and hurried to catch up with Marigold. They walked east on Forty-second Street like two stragglers from the First Crusade, Marigold with her helmet of hair and Thunder carrying the push broom perched on his right shoulder like the true cross.

The crusaders walked all the way to First Avenue and after asking nineteen people and getting their first answer from the nineteenth, turned left. The great gray and black buildings of the United Nations appeared before them splendidly tall and magic in their silhouette against the colorful, darkening sky.

Marigold was impressed. "Do you suppose," she said, "that they really *do* care?"

It was all too much for Thunder, who took a long pull from his wine bottle and politely offered it to Marigold.

"No, thank you," said Marigold turning down a drink for the first time in her life. "I'm speaking tonight."

Marigold and Thunder waited next to the "Swords Into Plowshares" monument until it was dark. She then took off her greatcoat, hid it under a stone bench where she could find it later, and unfolded the pink duster in her pocket and put it on, shivering in the Christmas cold. She looked at Thunder, who was holding his broom with both hands, and smiled. Her royal robe had become a cleaning lady's duster and together they looked like the folks from the cleaning service who had the lousy luck to have to work on Christmas Eve.

Without another word, they hurried across the street. Marigold, with her hands around her shoulders, was really cold and very convincing as she squealed "Merry Christmas!" to the guard at the gate and rushed on by him followed by Thunder holding the push broom out from his body at port arms.

Inside the entrance marked "Service" in several languages, Thunder found a cleaning cart with black wheels, full of plastic bottles, whisk brooms, and dust cloths. He laid his broom across the top of the cart and pushed it up a ramp, with Marigold bustling along behind, her hair covered with a fresh white dustcloth. The wide halls were dark and eerie, lit only by red Exit signs and an occasional small chandelier at the intersections.

They hurried along, a small pink cleaning caravan, winding through the corridors of power. There was not another soul to be seen on this Christmas Eve in the house of all the nations of the world.

It was the smell of freshly cleaned carpets that led them to the great Assembly Room. Thunder pushed open an enormous door and there, sweeping down before them like a graceful hillside, was the assembly chamber. It was filled with comfortable chairs and desks and aisles and small signs that said the names of countries, all leading on down to the podium, which sat on a small hilltop far away.

Marigold and Thunder stood in the doorway holding onto their cleaning cart and looked down the long and silent aisle. They were amazed.

"My God," said Marigold.

"You can say that again," said Thunder.

"My God," said Marigold.

With that, Marigold reached up and very carefully removed the dustcloth from her hair. Thunder thought she looked particularly beautiful at that moment. The great complicated hairdo had not fallen and it seemed as if, in the strange half light of the empty chamber, her pink duster had magically become a crimson robe and she looked like an African princess. You could see the strong bones in her face and the traces of royalty in her bearing.

Princess Marigold walked slowly down the aisle, trailing her robe and turning her head occasionally from side to side to acknowledge the silent applause of all the nations.

As she made her progress, Thunder abandoned the cleaning cart and ran down the other aisle looking for a place to sit. In the corner of his eye, he saw a familiar sign and made his way to the center of the hall and sat down in the middle of the Russian delegation. Once he was comfortable and had a substantial drink, he called out to Marigold.

"Better hurry up, old girl. Somebody's liable to run us out of here."

Marigold walked just a little faster and finally reached the steps up to the podium, which she ascended, walked past the famous tall white chair, and stood before the microphone. Above her hairdo was the huge silver symbol of the United Nations.

Marigold began, "Merry Christmas, everyone."

The microphone was off, but Marigold's voice, sounding like the thin reedy high notes of a harpsichord, penetrated the entire chamber. Thunder could hear every word.

"My name is Marigold and I'm very glad to be here. You have a wonderful warm room here, and Thunder and me are going to remember this day for the rest of our lives.

"There's a TV set in the window of the electronics store near where we live, and I try to watch the news each day and listen to the people who talk up here on this platform once in a while. Sometimes they say things they don't really mean, kinda like Thunder does when he's very drunk."

Thunder, from the Russian delegation, booed.

"Oh, me too!" said Marigold, "that's me all over, sayin' things I don't mean. I guess we all do that from time to time. The thing is that down on West Broadway, which is where we live, it doesn't make much difference what we do or what we say or whether we mean it or not. And I guess that's natural because we live outdoors and most folks think we're just about to die."

Marigold stopped. Shading her eyes, she looked out into the chamber for a moment.

"Can you hear me, Thunder? Is it okay so far?"

Thunder shouted back, "I can hear you, Marigold! You sound just fine!"

"Well," Marigold continued, "I got this idea that since I was always complainin' about the things you said up here, the only thing for me to do was to come on up and tell you how it is with us, because this is the United Nations and we're like a whole country all our own down on West Broadway and no one speaks for us.

"We have a funny country. The truth is it's not much of a country at all. We got no star-spangled banner, no flag or song. We don't shoot traitors and we've got no secrets that we keep. We don't even have an army or a war.

"And there's no place where our country ends! No edges anywhere. You know what I think? I think that every country in the world has another country just like us sittin' in its belly makin' trouble.

"We are, when you think about it, everywhere!"

Thunder hooped and applauded and Marigold paused and inclined her head slightly before she spoke again.

"Now, since we went to all this trouble to come up-town and ride the subway and fool the guards, I'm not gonna kid you. In my country there's a lot of problems. Willie Pendergast died last week and nobody said a word. They brought the emergency ambulance over to his grate and scraped him up like a fried egg, shoved him in the ambulance, and went away. The thing is, I didn't know Willie very well but I do know that his liver was down below his ribs and he felt a lot of pain. Now, the reason I'm telling you about Willie is that he didn't amount to much but he was like a lot of people in the world who don't amount to much but need someone to say their first and last names out loud before they die."

She paused sadly, then went on. "Willie, you know, only had one foot. The other was cut off or worn away somehow, but he actually managed to walk around except when he was very drunk and then he took the bandage off for sympathy and people went all the way across the street so they didn't have to pass a leper on their way to work.

"Now there's a lot of people who go across the street when they see Willie in their way. Maybe even millions and millions of people who don't want to look at Willie's foot without the bandage.

"And you're right, there's no excuse for Willie, and when you come right down to it there's no excuse for me. I guess we've made our bed and we should sleep in it.

"The problem is we just won't go away. Now that Willie's died, Thunder and me will take his grate, and when Thunder and me die, some poor soul with a story even sad-

148

der than mine will come along, feel the warm air comin' up from the subway steam pipe, and go to sleep.

"You see, my country is the end of the journey for a lot of people, and anyone who's born might come to live with us someday."

Marigold stopped for a moment. She was tired, but she took a deep breath, grabbed the podium on both sides, and summoned up the special words she'd saved.

"I know there are more important things to think about in your countries and I know about how you divide up God and fight about his prophets. But after you've talked about your prophets and your flags and stamped your feet to show how proud you are of who you are and where you're born, please let us in because it's cold, and Willie Pendergast, he froze to death."

Marigold was finished. She walked over and sat down in the tall white chair. Now Thunder was crying, and he walked on down the aisle and up the steps and knelt down so he could put his arm around her shoulder.

Thunder whispered, "It was beautiful, Marigold, just beautiful."

"Thank you."

"But the place was empty. No one heard it, only me."

"I guess that's just the point," said Marigold and smoothed her crimson robe across her knee.

The Devil in the Phoebe's Nest

JULIO PANDU WAS the devil. This was not an opinion but as hard a fact as you can find in the devil business. Harder, for example, than the argument Father Roger at St. Peter's Church might make for some sort of general devil who was everywhere, on the same level of ubiquity as God.

Julio had his devil office in the back room at E Pluribus Unum, a noisy saloon on Duane Street that had a small six-pocket pool table over which Julio presided with both venom and grace. Livingston Larrabee, one of the regulars at E Pluribus, once described Julio to the disappointed Mrs. Olivette as follows: "This young man, Mrs. Olivette, is a thief confessed . . . the most dangerous kind of person, a thief who *surrounds* his victims, an artful, ballet of a thief. With a suitable audience, a table, balls, and a stick, he can dance until the room is exhausted or, as some say, until someone dies."

Now that was quite a soaring indictment, particularly for Livingston Larrabee, who was a recovering alcoholic and given to 7UP and compensatory understatement. But you just *had* to soar when you talked about Julio Pandu. Mrs. Olivette, for example, normally an artless widow, noticed that, "Julio has a way with him. He glides through life. You know, I don't remember seeing him open a door. They just part like the Red Sea when he comes through." An outsider might wonder if Julio was one of *many* devils, and if not, why in the world would the devil operate out of a Tribeca bar? Where, one could reasonably ask, were the brimstone and mainframe computers that a modern devil would need to terrify and keep track of all the sinners in the world? Father Roger's concept of an omnipresent devil with an infinite number of offices made a lot more sense.

But there it was. Julio Pandu was the devil, the *only* devil, and if something treacherous happened in Sri Lanka he apparently could handle it between shots in an eight ball game in lower Manhattan.

Very few people knew that Julio was the devil. Livingston Larrabee didn't (although he *did* notice that his old craving for a dry martini returned whenever he was in the same room with Julio). Mrs. Olivette didn't. Indeed, the only people in the entire world who knew for sure that Julio was the devil were Marigold and Thunder.

It was Marigold's worldview, her ability to get immediately to the heart of things, that had led her to the United Nations and at the same time made her recognize Julio Pandu as the one and only devil in all the world.

Marigold's discovery was all the more impressive when you think of Julio's cover story. Julio was married, and his wife was Cassandra Pandu, a breathtakingly beautiful Jamaican woman who had no idea that her husband was anything other than a handsome pool hustler, a lousy provider, and a legendary adulterer. If Cassie Pandu (as she was called) had known that her husband was, in fact, the devil, she would have sighed a sigh of relief to find a simple explanation of his behavior.

Not knowing that Julio was the devil, Cassie had drawn her own conclusions and was casting about for a divorce. She had a new lover and was about to start her own business, a day-care center in her apartment that she had decided to call the Phoebe's Nest.

Now Julio, because he was the devil, knew about all this activity and wanted it stopped immediately, because although he needed a complicated modern American family as a front, he needed that family in place, not running around the divorce courts and making love to the neighbors.

Before I go any farther it is very important to understand some of the geography of this story. On the southwestern edge of Tribeca stand the two very tall towers of the World Trade Center. They stand on the foot of Liberty Street like two Protestant Cromwellian sentries overlooking the entire Tribeca community, their wintry gaze and shadow reaching all the way to the E Pluribus Unum pool room. Julio, understandably, did not like the World Trade Center.

Nor did Julio currently like Cassandra. He thought she was made of mush; full of sentiment and neighborly instincts that had led her to her latest folly, this Phoebe's Nest idea. On the few nights that Julio did come home, weary from his labors on the far side of the Styx, he hardly wanted a bunch of squalling bipeds in his living room.

So Julio had a number of problems that Thursday in December. In the first place it was Christmas Eve—again—exactly one year after Marigold and Thunder had made their journey north to the United Nations. (Although they had traveled alone and her speech had been delivered to an empty chamber, their odyssey had become a legend more secure in the neighborhood than the somber passage of Abraham Lincoln's body, in 1865, down Chambers Street and across the river to the Jersey railroad terminal. Thunder had seen to that. The image of Marigold, her hair almost taller than her person, standing in that august silence and pronouncing the creed of the poor was fixed like an equestrian statue in the community's mind.)

It was all just too damn much for Julio, who had spent the last nearly two thousand Christmases trying to sink the birthday of Jesus Christ in an ocean of retailing and prepubescent greed.

It also upset him that Marigold had peeked his card, knew he was the devil, and smiled a wicked smile at him every time he passed her grating on the way to E Pluribus Unum.

DOWN IN THE intestines of the World Trade Center, near the very place where a terrorist bomb had exploded in 1992, Richard Curry and Veronica Cross spent eight hours each day from noon until eight P.M. studying a great array of dials, the reading end of thousands of sensitive wires that snaked their way through the walls and floors of the great towers, even deep into the hard core of the Manhattan bedrock on which the buildings sat. This room, with its fluttering lights

and its bird noises (each instrument "chirped" in a different key), was the imperative result of the 1992 bombing.

Richard and Veronica's operating mode seemed just a
tad silly. They sat during most of their shift on two rolling
office chairs, propelling themselves around the room in a
sort of mating dance, much like two grasshoppers on cast-
ers, looking and listening to 167 sensing monitors.

The rules, which had been written by the head of the
Port Authority himself, called for Veronica or Richard to
check each of the monitors at least once an hour, a procedure that required plugging a skinny headphone into the face
of each instrument, listening to the appropriate *chirp*, and
reading the digital display. They would enter the readings
onto a preprinted form that indicated the normal range for
each instrument. The instruments diagnosed the building in
much the same way the monitoring station in a hospital
emergency room keeps track of the human body. Every con-
ceivable building function was monitored, the flow of the
air conditioners, the level of high pressure steam, the qual-
ity of the air, the wind speed, the condition of the auxiliary
generators, the tectonics of the bedrock supporting the
building, all electrical systems, and most dramatically, the
sway-ratio of the building itself.

The World Trade Center buildings each sway about
three feet on a normally windy day at the bottom of Manhattan. Sway-ratio numbers as high as eight feet had been
recorded over the years. Veronica, who had been on the job
two months longer than Richard, had actually monitored a

sway of nine feet two inches during a small hurricane. She had printed out and framed the startling graphic, and it hung above the sway-ratio monitor, blocking, incidentally, the screen of the bedrock vibration monitor that hadn't changed from a steady .00005 on the Richter scale in all the time the room had been in operation. Veronica almost always peeked under the framed picture to record the Richter numbers when she rolled by each hour.

By the way, the mating dance had served its role, and Veronica and Richard had finally become lovers two weeks before Christmas. It was all pretty sexy during working hours, as they whizzed about the room kissing and petting as they rolled past each other on the way to the next scheduled readout. On Christmas Eve, with seasonal enthusiasm, they had actually stopped rolling for a full two-minute embrace in the very middle of the room surrounded by their own Christmas display of winks and chirps and lights.

MEANWHILE, BACK IN her apartment in Tribeca Towers, Cassie Pandu was holding the first meeting of the Phoebe's Nest Cooperative. Her good friends Livingston Larrabee and Mrs. Jessie Olivette had agreed to serve on the Board of Directors, although Mrs. Olivette had originally been somewhat opposed to the plan because of her heroic view of Cassie, indeed her heroic view of most everyone.

"Well," Mrs. Olivette had said to one of Cassie's prospective customers, "Cassie Pandu would *never* sit children for money! Cassie Pandu is of the realm, royalty, an African princess; you can see it in her face."

Cassie had squashed that opinion quickly by asking Mrs. Olivette not to meddle. "That woman has four children and a rich husband," she told a chastened Mrs. Olivette.

"I'm so sorry I interfered," Mrs. Olivette had said. "It just seemed wrong, such a beautiful woman as you are, caring for children to make a few pennies. But I'm very sorry. I'll speak to her again."

"You needn't," Cassie had replied. "You complimented me, and that's a fine reference for the next time I see her."

So that was settled, and Jessie Olivette, widow of the Korean War hero Lt. Colonel Armstrong Olivette, would serve on Cassie's Board of Directors.

Cassie served tea.

The truth is that the other director at the meeting, Livingston Larrabee, Julio's eight ball victim and retired drunk, volunteered for the board because he was head over heels in love with Cassie Pandu. He despaired of fulfillment but found that he was enormously happy just to be in the same room with Cassie and found himself compulsively talking about profound matters whenever he was in Cassie's company. Before the formal meeting began, for example, Livingston, at the urging of Mrs. Olivette, had sailed into a discussion of bravery.

"A wonderful subject," Livingston said, teacup in hand. "Now that I'm growing old I am finally brave. Never before. To tell the truth, asleep or awake, my dreams were always cowardly. I was always swimming in great lakes of molasses toward some simple act of bravery, the opening of a door, the closing of a box. But even my mouth was plugged with syrup as I tried to say the manly things that would make my enemy angry.

"Until very recently, I have consoled myself by thinking of bravery as the currency of fools."

"I'm sure you're right, Livingston," interjected Cassie, "but I also believe Mrs. Olivette when she talks about her husband who was brave in battle and was much admired."

"Oh! Mr Larrabee!" interrupted Mrs. Olivette, "I have the letters, wonderful, awkward letters from young men who served with Mr. Olivette. I can bring them to you! You can read them out loud so that Cassie can hear them. They all say that Mr. Olivette was a brave lion of a man."

Livingston was briefly embarrassed. "Forgive me, Mrs. Olivette. I forget myself, wandering around in my head, thinking of times past, remembering how little I've done. I am a self-pitying fool, Mrs. Olivette, and I am impolite to Mr. Olivette." He raised his teacup, "Here, let's have a toast. To Mr. Olivette, your brave warrior!"

Cassie stood up and lifted her teacup, "And to the brave new Livingston Larrabee!"

"You know, it's true," said Mr. Larrabee, "and I've just found out. A young man on the subway jostled me and reached for my billfold. Without thinking, I snapped my elbow back into his stomach and I could hear the sound of his breath explode. He looked at me fearfully, gasping, and he moved away."

Mrs. Olivette's eyes were alight. "Did everyone applaud?"

"No one noticed," Livingston said solemnly. "Until now, it was a secret between that young man and me."

Cassie smiled. "A real secret, a real brave secret! Oh, how I miss you, Mr. Larrabee!"

Livingston was overwhelmed. He spoke softly, "To be missed by Cassandra Pandu . . ."

"Now," said Cassie, "tell us more about brave men."

Livingston sat down at the head of the table that had been organized for the meeting. "I think I have been careless with words for most of my life," Livingston began. "I changed the meaning of the word 'brave' because I was a coward. I've always talked of 'brave' ideas and 'brave' new worlds, but I meant something very different. Brave is nothing more or less than the simple act of courage, to walk into harm's way. It's just what it is, no more."

The two women looked at him with great respect.

"Well," said Livingston, "it's time we brought this meeting to order. First, we'll have a treasurer's report. Mrs. Olivette?"

Mrs. Olivette always found it hard to go from one thing to another. "Oh, Mr. Larrabee, you must give me a minute. I'm still thinking about bravery and knights of the Round Table and my own Mr. Olivette. I believe you've agreed that it is all right to be brave."

"It is indeed, Mrs. Olivette, although I've got my doubts about some of those knights who all believed they were going to go to heaven if they were killed in battle with the pagans. Since I don't believe in heaven, there is no reward for bravery on the IRT." He looked gently at Mrs. Olivette. "The treasurer's report, Mrs. Olivette, please."

"Well," said Mrs. Olivette, "we have one hundred and eleven dollars in the bank account and . . ."

Just at that moment, the teapot fell off the dining room table, the pictures on the wall rattled, and the room shuddered, much as Livingston's old dog, Dudley, would shake his whole body after falling in a lake.

Most everyone in downtown Manhattan felt the shudder. Marigold, sound asleep on her West Broadway grate, woke up a with a start and reached over to find Thunder who had rolled over on top of his wine bottle, which had broken in his street pajama pocket. The sweet smell of inexpensive wine floated upward.

Julio Pandu had just eyed a bank shot to sink the eight ball and win forty dollars from a fat stranger who had wandered innocently into E Pluribus Unum for a Christmas Eve afternoon glass of beer. The pool balls began to roll oddly back and forth across the table. As he was the devil, Julio immediately knew that a small earthquake had taken place and he decided to smile, weighing the natural catastrophe against the forty dollars he had lost.

Most important, down in the bottom of the World Trade Center, Veronica and Richard had been sneaking a peek at each other when they both rolled to a sudden halt as the picture covering the Richter scale crashed to the epoxy floor, sending shards of glass around the room. They rolled their way through the broken glass over to the monitor and found that the needle had scratched up a 2.8 reading from the rock directly below the World Trade Center.

Pete, the proprietor of Savannah Liquors, lost an entire shelf of White Lightning pints, one of the staples of the West Broadway community.

Generally speaking, there were smallish disasters, a broken ankle here, a plate of spaghetti in a raincoat pocket there, several spirited discussions between motorists who had bumped into one another, and a rash of burglar and car alarms going off, making a great and zany noise that was almost more than Thunder, with a raging hangover, could bear.

On an official level, all of the appropriate computers had snapped on. Policemen with new shiny helmets ran to designated emergency rooms with big yellow spots on the floor and stood, with their holsters unbuttoned, ready to handle anything.

But despite all the excitement, the general consensus was that New York City had been hit with a small, disconcerting tremor that was curiously focused almost entirely in the lower Manhattan area. Californians visiting New York, who happened to be in the affected area, were unanimously contemptuous of what they considered to be a negligible shiver.

Down in Veronica and Richard's monitoring room, however, it wasn't quite so simple. The Richter 2.8 tremor was, as they increasingly began to see it, symptomatic. Brief aftershocks produced a computer profile that popped out into Richard's hand. The profile indicated a 70 percent chance of further earthquakes of about the same or stronger intensity, in the same location. That, in itself, was not so worrisome, but across the room Veronica had ripped off a meteorological estimate from its roll, an estimate that showed gale-force winds surrounding a previously detected low out in the Atlantic that was moving directly toward the lower part of Manhattan island. As she stared at the circling isobars in her hand, an astounding and horrifying thought occurred to Veronica.

"Richard," she said softly.

"Not now," said Richard, misreading Veronica's sultry tone.

"Richard!" announced Veronica, and Richard snapped his head around.

"What happens," Veronica began slowly, "if gale-force winds, say a hundred miles an hour, strike the Trade Center *at the same moment* that a Richter three or larger earthquake moves the bedrock down below us."

Richard sat down. "The chances of that happening at the same time are about the same as my winning the lottery."

"Look at this." Veronica rolled over to Richard's side, handing him the meteorological tearsheet. "Did you put your lottery ticket in a safe place?"

AT THAT MOMENT, Julio Pandu of course knew the truth. As the devil, his sources were infallible. In exactly twenty-eight minutes and forty-four seconds, the winds from the Atlantic at 110 miles per hour and a major earthquake scoring 6.6 on the Richter scale would simultaneously strike both towers of the World Trade Center, and they would topple into the Tribeca community, the top floor of the North Tower arriving somewhere near E Pluribus Unum.

Now since Julio was the devil and had no character at all, the prospect of a major catastrophe with thousands dead or maimed on Christmas Eve was delicious. But his lack of character also meant that he could not keep a secret, and he was bursting to tell someone about the enormous crater that the World Trade Center would make in the middle of the neighborhood. But whom to tell? No one would believe him. Nobody knew he was the devil . . . except . . . of course! Marigold!

Julio raced around the corner to Marigold's grate and stood defiantly, hands on his hips, over Marigold and Thunder who were still recovering from the first tremor.

"That was nothing," intoned Julio.

"What's that supposed to mean?" replied Marigold fearlessly.

"In just about twenty-one minutes, old Marigold, the World Trade Center is going to fall over. Squash! Zap! Right on top of old Marigold!"

Thunder thought it was ridiculous. But Marigold gathered her blankets around her, stared straight ahead, and listened to the gathering wind whistling down West Broadway. "My God," she said.

Julio couldn't suppress a giggle. "You can forget about God, girl. He doesn't mess with natural phenomena. It's a policy position. He's had it for years. And I especially want you to know that I had *nothing* to do with this. Just an accident of nature," he added breezily.

Marigold struggled to her feet and looked right up Julio's nose. "Well," she said, "what are you going to do about it?"

"What am *I* going to do about it?" Julio laughed so loudly that it sounded like a peal of thunder. "Why, nothing! A whole bunch of nothing! That's what I'm gonna do."

Marigold's eyes narrowed (she was very good at narrowing her eyes). "I thought you *liked* it around here."

"I do! I do!" said Julio, slowing down, "I like it a lot. Sweet setup—gorgeous wife, ethnic mix, movie stars, plenty of sick homeless people, and, most of all, best of all, I *love* to shoot pool."

Marigold was suddenly mobilized. She saw everything clearly. The mantle of leadership had been thrust upon her once more. "Listen, Julio," she said in her most diplomatic tone, "will the Trade Center hit E Pluribus Unum?"

Julio fell silent. He imagined the enormous towers falling. Down and down they came, the two great iron sentries, crashing downward, the television tower on top of Tower 1 slicing through the roof of E Pluribus Unum and cutting the pool table in half.

"Damn!" said the devil.

Marigold struck. "It's all gonna be gone, the gorgeous wife, the perfect neighborhood, the pool table, all gone.

Your 'sweet setup' will be a bunch of smoke, Julio, a pile of trash. Unless . . ."

"Unless what?"

"Unless you stop it. Where is it written you can't mess with nature. You're not God, you know."

"Tell me about it," said Julio, musing, "I'd hate to miss a really terrible catastrophe, but I'm *used* to Cassie, except for that goddamn day-care center." He stopped. Considered.

"Tell you what," said Julio with a new enthusiasm. "I'll make you a deal!"

"A deal with the devil?" said Marigold.

"You betcha. An old-fashioned, slick-as-a-whistle, sell-your-soul-to-the-devil deal. We're talkin' precedent here, the usual contract—you give me your soul, and I stop the hurricane and the earthquake."

"That's not the usual deal," said Marigold. "Where's the part about me getting rich, eating truffles, and sleeping with Clark Gable?"

Thunder was upset, but all he could think of was, Clark Gable's dead.

Julio looked at his watch. It was an affectation; he always knew what time it was. "In the first place, you've got seventeen minutes to make up your mind, and in the second place, I don't want *your* soul, you'd probably organize hell. . . ."

Marigold was relieved. "Whose, then?"

Julio smiled his most malevolent smile. "Livingston Larrabee and Jessie Olivette. The Board of Directors of the Phoebe's Nest!"

DOWN IN THE World Trade Center, the bottom dwellers, Richard and Veronica, had made six phone calls, each call to a higher authority. By the time she reached the mayor's assistant, Risky Lafferty (his odd first name the result of a near miss with a broken condom in high school), she was screaming, "Evacuate Tribeca! Goddamn it, Risky, the sway-ratio meter is already reading seven feet!"

"Veronica?" asked Risky. "Is that you, Veronica?"

"You bet your ass it's me, you incompetent son of a bitch!"

"Do you know you're sexy when you're mad?"

"I'm talking about the goddamn World Trade Center. It's gonna fall over, and you, you asshole, are sitting four miles north!"

"Now calm down, Veronica, it's not gonna fall over. I asked the mayor!"

Veronica slammed down the phone and then turned to Richard. "Nobody believes us," she said wearily.

The sway-ratio meter stuttered past eight and headed for nine.

OUTSIDE THE ENTRANCE of Tribeca Towers, Marigold, Julio, and Thunder leaned into the powerful wind and struggled through the glass doors. There was something about the look in Marigold's eyes that convinced the doorman that they should pass through the lobby unchallenged and into the elevator. Marigold was peeking at Julio's watch. "Thirteen minutes," she said.

"Twelve minutes, forty seconds," said Julio without looking.

They got out at the twenty-ninth floor and buzzed the buzzer at 29J. Cassie Pandu left her guests seated at the dining room table and went to the door.

Marigold and Thunder burst into the room, both talking at the same time. "There's only twelve minutes left!" said Marigold to the startled Board of Directors.

"You gotta sell your soul," shouted Thunder at Livingston Larrabee. Then he pointed at Mrs. Olivette, "And you too!"

Mrs. Olivette gasped and fell backward over Cassie's embroidered footstool. Livingston Larrabee rushed to help her up.

"Look what you've done," said Livingston Larrabee. "You've frightened Mrs. Olivette!"

Marigold was almost hysterical. Pointing at Julio, she began, "He . . . he's . . . he's the devil!"

"So what else is new, Marigold," said Cassie. "Why don't you take the devil back to E Pluribus Unum and out of my house!"

"*Your* house? *Your* house?" shouted Julio, and he vaulted into the center of the room. Waving his arms and stomping on the rug, Julio did a slippery, snaky devil dance, as he pointed at the window. "I'll show you what's going to happen to *your* house." He slimied up close to the window.

"That building over *there* is going to fall down on this building over *here*."

"No it's not!" yelled Marigold, and then her voice was suddenly purposeful and firm, "a deal is a deal!"

Livingston Larrabee, always the statesman since he stopped drinking, called for order and turned to the grim-faced Marigold. "Now, Marigold, I think you owe us an explanation."

Marigold sat heavily in the big chair—Thunder automatically took his place at her side, sitting on the floor—and began, "There's not much time, and it's a long story. In the first place, he *is*," pointing at Julio, "the devil."

DEEP IN THE bowels of the earth, down in the monitor room, Veronica and Richard were slowly disrobing each other.

As she flung Richard's old-fashioned shoulder strap undershirt across the room, Veronica said, "What the hell, Richard, take me! The sway-ratio is eleven feet!"

Richard giggled and Veronica pulled down his boxer shorts.

MEANWHILE, MARIGOLD HAD finished. She had explained the whole story. Now she looked up at Livingston Larrabee.

Livingston spoke evenly, bravely, "Now let me get this straight. In eight minutes—"

169

"Make that six," interrupted Julio.

"In six minutes," continued Livingston, "the World Trade Center is going to fall over on top of Tribeca. Julio is the devil and is willing to stop the disaster if Mrs. Olivette and I will sell him our souls."

"Right," said Marigold.

"Exactly," said Thunder.

"Outstanding," said Julio.

"Bananas," said Cassie. "The whole thing is ridiculous. Now I'd be the first to say that Julio is no prince among men, but the devil? He's a jerk, a wimp, a no-good pool-hustling parasite, but the devil? Don't be ridiculous."

All eyes turned to Julio. He was furious. "You wanna see devil! *You wanna see devil?*" And he turned Cassie into an enormous kiwi bird, munching on plate of worms in the middle of the dining room table.

Down in the monitor room, it looked as if a great, historic, triple-header was going to happen. The sway-ratio passed fifteen feet as the wind velocity passed one hundred miles an hour, and folks inside the two buildings were beginning to notice office chairs racing around the room on their own and flowerpots upending on the secretaries' desks. Deep in the earth, far below the room where Veronica and Richard were entwined, two great tectonic plates strained against each other, about to pop in two minutes, the exact moment that the wind, Veronica, and Richard would reach their climax.

Back up in Cassie's apartment, Mrs. Olivette, mindful of her role as the widow of a winner of the Congressional Medal of Honor, kept her composure, patted Cassie's huge hairy, wingless flank, and said to Julio, "Where do I sign?"

"Here." Julio thrust a blue-backed contract on legal-sized paper and a wet feather pen into her hands. Mrs. Olivette put the contract down on the table next to the plate of worms and signed. Julio turned to Livingston Larrabee, who had lost it when Cassie turned into a kiwi. Livingston babbled with fear, "What should I do? Oh, Mrs. Olivette, what should I do?"

"Sign," said Mrs. Olivette.

"Thirty seconds," said Marigold and Julio at the same time.

"It was a lie!" Livingston burst out, "it was a fantasy. That kid on the subway got my wallet. I was terrified. I spent three weeks replacing the credit cards."

"Sign," said Mrs. Olivette.

"Ten seconds," said Marigold and Julio.

The tectonic plates began to slip, the sway increased to eighteen feet, and a smile began to blossom on Veronica's face.

"Seven," said Julio.

"Six," said Marigold.

"Five," said Thunder.

"Four," said Mrs. Olivette.

"Kee! Wee!" said Cassie Pandu.

Livingston signed.

"Ahyeeeee!" cried Veronica.

"Wow!" said Richard as the earth did not move.

And the wind died down.

And the towers stood tall on Christmas Day.

171

Redemptions

MARIGOLD UNDERSTOOD THE paradigms. A thousand unusual things could happen and she would stubbornly fill her bent aluminum cup with Thunder's warm wine and drink deeply, letting the wave of it wash through her.

And then, at another time, a single thing—the bend of the wind around Morgan's grocery, or an extra cough from Agnes—could bring Marigold to full alert and a whole program would fall in place. Detailed planning and diplomatic options would materialize and Marigold would again be master of the great currents of our time.

It all began in late December when Marigold was sitting on her West Broadway grate idly looking down through the bars for nickels, dimes, and shiny trinkets. She looked up and saw a muffled platoon of strangers, dressed up as homeless people, marching down Chambers Street. They each carried an enormous bag of aluminum cans and they moved with a measured tread toward Greenwich Street, where they turned right and headed toward the Food Emporium.

Marigold could immediately tell that these were not really homeless people because under their tattered coats, hats, and shaggy pants there were fancy earmuffs, turtlenecks, and woolen stockings peeking out.

At first she thought that somebody was making a

movie in the neighborhood, but there were no cameras or mobile homes full of fuzzy people, and, to be sure, another lot of "homeless" people appeared two hours later, making the same silent progress toward the supermarket.

"I'd been wondering," said Marigold to Thunder, "where the cans had gone. For weeks, everybody's been complaining that they are harder and harder to find. And then these strangers start marching through the neighborhood, carrying thousands and thousands of them. Something very strange is going on."

Not much was sacred on West Broadway except the cans. By an accident of history, the environmental spasm of the 1960s and 1970s had produced a world full of redeemable aluminum cans that in turn produced a small but certain income for the folks on West Broadway. The cans were like an intravenous flow into the pockets and stomachs of the desperately poor.

So Marigold asked around.

Mrs. Lochinvar, the night manager at the Food Emporium (who was a lot nicer than the day manager), beckoned Marigold outside where they held a whispered conversation next to the green Dumpster.

"I figure," whispered Marigold, "that my folks ordinarily get maybe one or two percent of the cans that you sell. We pick 'em sticky out of the trash baskets and the gutters and even grab a few from the recycle bins, but nobody makes more than a few bucks a week. Even those have disappeared."

She leaned close to Mrs. Lochinvar and lowered her voice even further, "Who are these people, Mrs. Lochinvar, who are stealing my cans?"

When she said, "Stealing my cans!" Marigold suddenly waved her arms and raised her voice so loud that Mrs. Lochinvar was genuinely alarmed and pulled Marigold into the stairway that leads into the garage and closed the door.

In the dark enclosure, Mrs. Lochinvar spoke. "The Presbyterians," she said.

"The what?" asked a startled Marigold.

"The Presbyterians," Mrs. Lochinvar repeated.

"I'll be damned." said Marigold.

"Don't say that!" exploded Mrs. Lochinvar.

"That's ridiculous," said Marigold, "those nice, straight-up-and-down white people with their linen napkins and their terrible swift God, they don't collect cans! God forbid!"

LESS THAN AN hour later, Marigold and Thunder had climbed the marble steps of the grand Presbyterian church on Church Street and were sitting on a hard back bench with Associate Pastor Fustian, who, far from being straight up-and-down, was wider than he was tall.

The pastor listened to Marigold most soberly and then began to puff and twinkle, "Redemption," smiled the pastor, "is a serious business."

"You're telling me," replied Marigold, ignoring the

theology. "Billie made twenty-three dollars one week and spread it around. We all had roast beef sandwiches. . . ."

"I got some Wild Irish Rose," added Thunder, "good stuff!"

"Young man," thundered the pastor, adjusting his beam to the pew, "you have found the evil praxis of the drunkard!"

"Amen," said Thunder, and the pastor twinkled once again.

Dr. Fustian cleared his throat and looked toward the great spartan altar of the church.

"Here, in the presence of our savior," began Dr. Fustian, intoning at first but slowly slipping into a sort of sweet, narrative voice, "I will tell you, Marigold, that you have stumbled across one of the great Christian calamities of our time."

"I have?" said Marigold, elbowing Thunder lightly in the ribs.

"You have indeed," said Dr. Fustian. "I have, for most of my life," he continued, "been troubled by the shattered vessel of modern Christianity." Dr. Fustian was given to high metaphor and other soaring figures of speech. He paused several seconds and then added, in great confidence, "I have, in fact, immodestly seen myself as the healer of the great Christian schisms."

He paused again before saying, "and then . . ."

Dr. Fustian lumbered to his feet, waddled to the altar, disappeared for a moment into the sacistry, and then struggled up the stairs of the center pulpit with a Diet Sprite can in his right hand.

". . . came Environmental Law 27-1003."

"Our can law?" called Marigold. She was now sitting fully forty feet from Dr. Fustian, who was surrounded, as he would put it, by the dark mahogany of three hundred years.

"The can law!" bellowed Dr. Fustian, and he raised the Diet Sprite can above him so that the winter sun bounced off its silver top. Dr. Fustian had become a fat Christmas tree with a glinting aluminum star.

"Well, I never," said Marigold.

"Me either," added Thunder.

"The ecumenical can!" pronounced Dr. Fustian. "After a century of searching for the common ground, it happened—we agreed!"

"To what?" asked Marigold.

"To a joint project! A partnership! To act in concert! To be, as it were, on the same biblical page!"

"Wonderful," said Marigold.

But Dr. Fustian was not to be denied. "No more transubstantiation debates, no more guitars on the altar. Peace, peace at long last."

He lowered the can and floundered his way back to the bench where Marigold and Thunder were sitting. Exhausted, his breath popped out of his mouth like white lace doilies in the chilly Presbyterian room.

"Colder in here than it is out there!" exclaimed Thunder, who twirled his burlap muffler twice around his neck and took a decent-sized drink without looking at the altar.

Finally, Dr. Fustian caught his breath. He raised his stubby fingers to his mouth as if ashamed. "But I have failed," he said.

"How?" said Marigold.

"Turn up the thermostat," suggested Thunder, trying to be helpful.

"I brought them all together, here in this room."

He jumped up and polkaed down the aisle again, a Pickwickian dance. "It was my finest hour! I had it all! Local Law Eighty-three had been penned in heaven. At the end of this horrid, televised, born-again era with crystal cathedrals and pornographic ministries I could at last fill the poor boxes, balance the Presbyterian checkbook, borrow the Episcopalian's broker . . . in a word, detente. I could," he paused in the dance, "put Christianity in the black."

Marigold began to cry. "Why am I crying, Dr. Fustian?"

"You are crying, Marigold, because you are a great and sensitive woman."

"Then why," asked Marigold, cutting to the heart of the matter, "did you steal our cans?"

"God's cans, Marigold, God's cans," ignored the pastor.

"I decided on a pilot project," he rushed onward, "a neighborhood conference of all the churches, including the Catholics. It was in the dark dead of night, and *everyone* was here in this very room. Even the local priest came and he brought a man with a pocket calculator. A slightly worn Methodist with a Swiss accent arrived, and the Baptists sent a small quartet who broke out into song during the breaks.

"The Unitarians, Episcopalians, and Congregationalists arrived on small motorcycles.

"But the grandest miracle of all was the fortuitous arrival of Franklin Frothbone, an ancient Presbyterian and inventor, reputed to be a descendant of John Knox himself. Mr. Frothbone, easily one hundred years of age, came to the meeting with detailed blueprints and specifications for the world's first industrial-sized *aluminum* magnet, which, if suspended from a hot-air balloon, would suck up all of the aluminum cans in a fifty-yard radius. Mr. Frothbone had intended to sell his invention to the United States government, but in a dazzling ploy to God he sought redemption in his final moments by turning this magnificent device over to me."

Pastor Fustian sat down, exhausted. But he was soon revived. "From then on it was easy. We put all theology aside and talked trucks and warehouses, massive simony on a scale that would have frightened a Borgian pope. We worked out details, arranged for the assembly of the magnet, purchased a hot-air balloon from a bankrupt carnival, assigned hotels and apartment houses to each faith, and as the dawn arrived the next morning behind the Brooklyn Bridge, the delegates broke through these great double doors and raced to their tasks, filled with the fire and blessing of a debt-free future."

Despite himself, Thunder was excited, "What happened?"

Dr. Fustian's tongue curled out of his mouth and wet his lips before he spoke. "Margaret Pegleg Malmsey" he said darkly, "that's what happened."

"Oh, my God!" Thunder exploded.

MARGARET MALMSEY, KNOWN as "Peggy" or "Pegleg," was a mighty presence in the neighborhood.

First of all, people could set their watch by the hollow *clonk!* that Peggy made when she took her morning constitutional on the cobblestones of Harrison Street. Her right leg was an aluminum pole with a plastic bottom that acted as a mouthpiece to a resonating chamber when she walked, or rather marched home from work each morning. She made her morning progress across Harrison Street because she loved to wake up the community with her cobblestone *clonk, clonk, clonk* echoing through the great Greenwich Towers at six A.M. And who, indeed, was going to stop her, a fiery-faced old John Brown of a woman with an aluminum leg and a clump of hair growing out of her right cheek.

For all her strange appearance, Peggy was a computer genius. Each night, starting at the stroke of midnight, she would swing into her great Queen Anne chair in the center of the American Express computer control room in the tall American Express Building on the north end of Greenwich Street. She would unscrew her leg and place it in a specially made velveteen-lined nook and proceed to unscramble the arcane languages and subtle frenzies that governed the machines that, in turn, governed millions of transactions, credit cards, letters of credit, stock and bond purchases, sales, and all the other capital soup of our society. At exactly five minutes to six each morning, she would screw her leg back on, clear the screens for the new day's work, and set out to clonk her way up and down Harrison Street, eventually heading home to the shabby Bond Hotel on West Broadway where she was both a resident and the owner.

When she arrived at the hotel, the Professor, who served as her night manager, would, if he was sufficiently sober, report to Peggy the night's admissions, which were usually listed on a yellow legal pad as "Melody R., Room 4, $3.00" and so on with the penmanship deteriorating toward the bottom as the Professor polished off his fourth pint bottle.

Actually, Peggy Malmsey (her great-grandfather had named himself after the Greek wine in which the duke of Clarence was drowned) had had a great deal of money and a great many sins. "Seven figures and goes straight to hell" was the word on the street. Her arrangement with American Express was in fact a kind of high-tech blackmail. Peggy's absolute control of the entire AMEX software culture meant that with a single application in the middle of the night, Peggy would routinely save the corporation millions of dollars and was thus also positioned to wreak havoc on the bottom line of the financial behemoth.

They paid her extremely well.

Like most powerful people, Peggy was terrified of

God. Winding through her dark machinations was a thread of terror for her sins. She honestly believed that God looked just like her and had painted all her mirrors black so that she did not have to look at her maker after she had completed some damnable, hurtful plan.

By the way, poverty was not one of Peggy's eccentricities. In the lobby of the shabby, transient Bond Hotel, she had installed an elevator that was masked by a rack of pornographic magazines. Behind a well-thumbed copy of *Penthouse*, there was a button that, when depressed, opened the wall to a sumptuous elevator with a blue satin reclining couch on which Peggy would drape herself each morning at seven after she had completed her business with the Professor. The elevator would rise, playing "Love's Old Sweet Song," to the fourteenth floor of the Bond Hotel where Peggy's full-floor penthouse spread out before her. It was a great nest of Victorian stuffed birds and flowered upholstery with endless connecting rooms in which great rectangular canvases were displayed showing scenes of waterfalls and autumn forests in gilded, sculpted frames. Here and there a marble cupid stood on the thick Arabian carpets, drawing a stony bead with his bow and arrow on various chief executive officers when they came to pay their respects.

"WELL," SAID PASTOR Fustian, back at the Presbyterian church talking to Marigold and Thunder, "we were in business less than a month. Our great pink and purple balloon with its heavenly magnet spiriting cans to its bosom was a great success, except for the occasional hood ornament or aluminum chamber pot that came to join the cans.

"The balloon then dumped its cargo in our Hubert Street warehouse and a small army of unemployed actors dressed as homeless people carried large plastic bags of the redeemable cans to selected supermarkets. We rotated supermarkets so that no one supermarket would be overwhelmed. The actors kept twenty percent of the redemption, and the rest of the money was collected by a committee of accountants that included all of the various religions, who kept an eye on one another.

"In four weeks we had paid off the balloon and were making ten thousand dollars a week clear profit in this neighborhood alone! I was about to bring the matter to the attention of highest officials of each faith, when the phone rang and we were doomed."

"Peggy?" asked Marigold.

"Peggy," confirmed Dr. Fustian.

"It seems that she had got wind of our operation. The warehouse is right across the street from her office, so she punched us up on her computers and discovered that old-fashioned Christianity has been operating on the gossamer of plastic credit for years.

"I can just see her, with that crooked smile making the hair on her face wiggle, punching up the Presbyterians and all the others, calling in the debt. They started padlocking churches, repossessing the poor boxes, garnisheeing the collection. It was a nightmare!

"Finally, she called us all to a meeting in that bordello of hers and offered to call it off if we gave her the can business; actors, balloon, even the magnet.

"We surrendered." Pastor Fustian buried his face in his hands, sobbing. "We surrendered," he whispered through his tears.

"Now, now," said Marigold, rising to her full height and putting a comforting hand on Pastor Fustian's bald head, "Thunder and me, we'll take care of everything."

"Everything?" whimpered the Pastor. "But how? How!" he shouted. "She controls it all. She has the keys to the kingdom. *She understands the software!*"

"Never mind," said Marigold, taking the squashed Diet Sprite can from the pastor's trembling grasp, "it'll be all right."

And with that, Marigold put the can in her pocket, swept Thunder to his feet, and sailed out the double doors. Her face gleamed with her new mission. But as she walked down to the corner, she looked back over her shoulder at the pastor, who stood bewildered in the doorway.

"You forgot about us, Dr. Fustian. Everyone, everywhere, always forgets about us," called out Marigold as she and Thunder scuttled north on Church Street.

The next morning, when Peggy Malmsey clonked into the lobby of the Bond Hotel and poked the Professor awake with her plastic foot, he handed her the usual yellow paper. At the bottom, Peggy could barely make out "Marigold and Thunder in the Penthouse."

"In the *penthouse!*" Peggy roared.

The Professor startled all the way up to a standing position and blubbered, "But they're my friends."

"Those scruffy bums!" Peggy retorted. "Never mind." And she pushed the *Penthouse* lady's navel and the elevator doors opened magestically.

Up in Peggy's landscape of Victorian lumps and curves, Thunder thought he had died and gone to heaven. Upon opening a large credenza, he discovered a cache of brown, green, and clear glass bottles containing every distilled and fermented liquid in the history of man. Their dazzling, beckoning labels spoke to him in a dozen languages. The collective smell seemed to him almost Arabian, and Thunder felt he would be transported to a better, more beautiful world if only he could consume it all. As he stood there, he reached in his belt, grasped his warm bottle of Thunderbird wine, raised it solemnly above his forehead, and drank a silent, respectful toast.

Marigold had settled down in what appeared to be the throne room. At one end of the long room lined with black-painted mirrors there was a large puffed-up blue velvet loveseat on a platform. Punctuating the velvet were yellow brocade buttons, and in the middle of the back of the loveseat a large wooden Maltese cross grew out of the top of Marigold's head when she took her seat in the exact center.

"Get your fat ass out of my chair," thundered Peggy Malmsey as she strode from her elevator, past the mesmerized Thunder, and through the enormous door that opened in to the far end of the throne room.

"Margaret!" replied Marigold, "behave yourself!" Marigold had used the form of Peggy Malmsey's name that no one had uttered in a quarter century.

Peggy stopped dead still in the center of the room.

The moment should have been frozen in time and placed in a magical archive with the meeting of Napoleon and Czar Alexander 1 in the middle of the Nemen River. The two grande dames of Tribeca, each representing a powerful army, stood face to face: Marigold, undisputed queen of the homeless, and Peggy, Medea of the computers.

The hair on Peggy's cheek stood straight out as the blood rose up past her nose to the top of her head. She was so outraged she could not speak.

"Margaret," repeated Marigold, "it's time we had a talk."

"About what!" Peggy was virtually screaming.

"About the cans."

"What cans?"

"Don't mess with me," said Napoleon. "You can mess with everybody in the world except me and my people. We want the can business back." She took the Diet Sprite can out of her pocket and tossed it across the room. It landed on a stuffed ostrich.

Czar Alexander snarled, "Why should I listen to a bunch of scraggly losers?" She was recovering, "Bums, tramps, parasites, drunks, and lunatics! Get out of my house!" She pointed distastefully at Thunder, "And take your rummy with you!"

Marigold rose to her full height and walked to the center of the room, standing six inches away from Peggy. Nose to nose, she spoke with a whispering eloquence, "You'll listen to us because . . ." she paused, "because we got no credit!" Marigold cackled up a great laugh, "We got *no* credit at all. We're not even in the system. You can close down the Presbyterians, you can mess with the Methodists, but you can't break us. We're already broke!"

"Out!" screamed Peggy Malmsey. "Out, bitch!"

"Come on, Thunder," said Marigold. She marched into the elevator, draped herself across the couch, and with Thunder pushing the buttons, descended.

BACK AT THE Presbyterian church, Pastor Fustian was riddled with guilt. Marigold's parting shot had awakened the old humility of his Puritan forefathers and he cast about for some way to redeem himself in Marigold's eyes and at the same time recapture the cans. The answer came to him as a vision that appeared in the form of a Cary Grant caper movie.

Late that night, the pastor was down in the subbasement of the church trying to put on a black rubber catsuit that he had bought that afternoon at a Nassau Street shop that specialized in frisky costumes. He stuffed himself into the catsuit, but he couldn't close the final zipper, leaving a large, flesh-colored oval spot on his back. His original plan was to cross the roofs like a jewel thief, all the way over to the Hubert Street warehouse where the balloon was kept, steal the balloon, and then fly over to the Bond Hotel for a penthouse confrontation with Pegleg Malmsey.

Everything went wrong. In the first place, he took a cab to Hubert Street when he found that he could barely walk, much less run, across the rooftops. When he got to the warehouse, the door was locked and he had to flop himself through a window to reach the room where the balloon was stored. The balloon was collapsed into a great pile of pink and purple vinyl next to a wicker basket, a butane hot-air torch, and the famous magnet.

He dragged everything into the street, stretching out the balloon and connecting the basket, the torch, and the magnet. Then he discovered that he didn't have a match and had to go all the way to the all-night Korean grocery where the proprietor gave an entire carton of matches to the black apparition with the pink spot.

The brave pastor, match in hand, climbed into the wicker basket and lit the butane torch. The balloon slowly inflated, rising in the cold night air until an untimely gust of wind snatched the balloon and took the pastor to West Orange, New Jersey.

Meanwhile, Marigold and Thunder were organizing. It took all of the next afternoon to gather everyone in the street outside the beauty shop window. Thunder had constructed a small platform made of wooden pallets from

Bazzini's, and Marigold with some difficulty (her right foot had been numbing up as winter came on) climbed up on the platform.

She looked out across a great junkyard of people in tattered fedoras and old khaki army blankets, galoshes, and burlap. Agnes was dressed in a tablecloth; Fred sported a sailor suit and waved a feather duster. Here and there a bright pink artificial tulip popped out of a raggedy clump of hair. The Salvation Army band with the tarnished buttons and a bent trombone set out its bucket and tripod and played "Nearer My God to Thee." Shouts of "Hi Marigold!" and "What's up Marigold?" rose above the brassy music. The merry smell of cheap wine braced the air as at least three hundred sets of eyes turned toward Marigold.

Marigold raised her hands for silence and Thunder enforced it by pointing his finger at noisemakers. The band ended abruptly in the middle of a phrase, and it was entirely quiet except for the distant honk of cars on West Street and an occasional toot from a boat on the river.

"Thank you. Thank you for coming," Marigold began.

"Louder!" "Down in front!" replied everybody.

Thunder sternly put his hands on his hips.

"We got trouble," said Marigold, and a roar of laughter went up.

"Tell me about it!" shouted Agnes from under her tablecloth.

"No, I mean *big* trouble. Trouble with the cans!"

This time, there was a murmur that rose to a full angry roar. This was life and death.

Agnes spoke up, "There's been hardly any cans for weeks. . . ."

Fred announced, "I saw those bums on Hubert Street, and they had plenty of cans . . . marchin' along."

"Those ain't bums!" Marigold replied, "they're actors and they're workin' for Peggy Malmsey. Peggy Malmsey is stealing our cans!"

There was a stunned silence. And during the silence, far away, the crowd heard a distant *clonk, clonk* on Harrison Street.

"It's her!" shouted Frank as he fell to his knees whimpering, "what are we gonna do?"

"We're gonna take back our cans!" shouted Thunder. He and Marigold jumped from the wooden pallet platform and headed north toward Harrison Street.

The motley pack of homeless people followed. Up West Broadway they marched, taking a left on Duane Street and curving en masse up Greenwich toward Harrison, where Peggy Malmsey stood alone in the center of the street.

Peggy had a large whistle in her mouth and blew it loud and shrill as Marigold and her friends surged toward her.

Filing out of the side streets from both directions came the actors, dozens of them, and they formed a phalanx behind Peggy. Each one had been bribed with an American Express card with a two-hundred-dollar credit line, and they became a formidable army with their bulging bags of cans set down before them across the entire width of Greenwich Street.

Marigold's raggedy mob stumbled to a halt. Fifty feet

separated the two armies. Thunder was standing behind Marigold, urging her forward.

"Go get 'em, old girl," said Thunder, and the two women advanced toward each other in solemn steps.

Suddenly, a great honking sound came from high above. And there, far above Greenwich Street, high above the two shabby armies, was a great pink and purple hot-air balloon with Pastor Fustian in his black rubber suit standing in the basket. He was squeezing a rubber honker horn in one hand and holding a bullhorn in the other. The enormous and infernal magnet hung from the basket, and as the balloon descended it whacked into the asphalt street between the two armies.

Pastor Fustian, a great black blob of a heavenly apparition, spoke into the bullhorn, and his voice rattled the windows all along the street. "I say unto thee," he shouted in the sudden silence, "that the cans belong to the people! Love one another! It is the season of redemption. It is Christmas once again!"

Whereupon the actors and Marigold's people all broke ranks and ran to each other, dumping their cans, embracing and kissing, dancing and rollicking as the Salvation Army Band started to play, adding to the madness and joy of it all.

A small hill of aluminum cans and plastic bottles began to rise in the center of Greenwich Street, soon becoming a great sticky mountain. The people joined hands and danced in a grand circle around it.

The pastor, who was secretly astonished at the success

of his admonition, called again for silence, raised his arms in the air, and spoke, "Margaret Malmsey!"

Peggy looked up, saw the God of her nightmares, and quickly fell to her knees.

(In truth, as he spoke, the pastor was frantically holding his rubber suit together as it began to separate from the point of the broken zipper.)

"Margaret Malmsey," he repeated, "you are apostate!"

He then lost his balance and flopped head over heels from the basket. Marigold and Thunder gathered him up.

The pastor looked Peggy Malmsey in the eye. "You will give us back our cans!"

It was all to much for Peggy Malmsey, God appearing from the sky and all.

She said a most remarkable thing. "Merry Christmas," said Peggy Malmsey, in a soft and not unfriendly voice.

"Merry Christmas," said both the pastor and Marigold.

Four members of the Salvation Army band had stepped into the basket, and the balloon began to lift majestically again.

"Merry Christmas!" shouted everybody.

Above, the sounds of a very small brass quartet playing "Silent Night" were punctuated with the *ping* and *clonk* of the aluminum cans as they arrived at Mr. Frothbone's magnet after flying through the midnight clear.

Fourteen Days of Marigolds

Tuesday, October 24, Day One

Most of Marigold's friends had one and one half shirts, could expect to live an additional two to four years, and had a median annual income of three hundred and eleven dollars.

So, for those social workers who were always stopping by her grate on West Broadway urging her to "Organize!" she would reach over and slide Thunder's pint bottle of Wild Irish Rose out from behind his pink waistband sash and toast the intruder with the following: "Just keep me on your Rolodex, Anastasia. The homeless will rise first thing Monday morning."

Marigold had produced enough paperwork at the Department of the Homeless and various other good-doing agencies to provide the basis for a small hill of undergraduate papers, master's theses, and doctoral dissertations.

Both social workers and academics secretly wanted Marigold to remain where she was forever. She was a great meadow of marigolds that everybody could romp in during working hours, concocting theories and writing grant proposals.

Everybody, that is, except Flash Gordon.

"You know what you are?" sassed Flash one cool October afternoon to a sleepy-eyed Marigold. "You're a goddamn role model, the perfect bum, the vagabond, the all-time tramp."

"Everybody's gotta be someplace," answered Marigold.

"Well, I think you oughta improve yourself and run for mayor," said Flash.

Byron Lord Gordon, known as "Flash," was a press agent who affected a black fedora and an old-fashioned long-sleeved white shirt, clean each day. By arriving at the civil rights movement directly from the publicity department of Metro-Goldwyn-Mayer in the 1960s, he had carved out a special niche in the PR universe. He was the street-smart flack who had one foot planted in Marigold's world and the other up in Hurley's saloon, a high-tone media hangout tucked into the southwest corner of Rockefeller Plaza.

Although she genuinely liked Flash, Marigold was not pleased by Flash's proposal. It was not the first time someone had suggested politics to Marigold; she was, after all, New York City's most noble savage. When in his cups Flash would call her "Sitting Bull," and the parallels to the great Lakota Sioux were not so far-fetched. Like Sitting Bull, Marigold had, on at least two occasions, brought together a loose confederation of her tribes for a great activity—once prior to her appearance at the United Nations and a second time at the Battle of Greenwich Street in the Great Can War.

Because Flash made the suggestion, Marigold felt it was required of her to make a proper answer. So she said, "It's nice of you to think of me, Flash. It's nice that you don't think it's plain silly for an old mop like me to better herself. But Thunder and me, we live in a small, protected place on earth, and when we step outside that place we might begin to die."

"I'll take that as a maybe, Marigold," said Flash with enthusiasm. "After a couple of straw polls, some campaign songs, and a look at the bathrooms in Gracie Mansion, you might just change your mind."

Marigold untangled from her army blanket and came to a standing position with Thunder reaching up and supporting her left leg, the one that had been numbing up recently. It was, for a moment, the old regal Marigold as the army blanket arced through the air and came to rest across her chest.

"I am content," said Marigold, "to sip wine in the sun, take care of Thunder, and do no disservice to my fellow man."

Flash Gordon made notes and left.

THE TRUTH IS that Burton "Benny" Brazil had been mayor for much too long.

His first couple of terms (after handily beating Arnold Bender, known on the streets as "Bleeding Heart" Bender or just "the Bleeder") were whiz-bang fresh and exciting, catching the fancy of the electorate with red suspenders, take-out Chinese food, and a task force that succeeded in making the Hudson River sewage disposal plant opposite Harlem smell nice by buying and dispensing four and a half billion cubic feet of Autumn Breeze air freshener.

But Benny Brazil's just-plain-folks style got to be a bore after a while, particularly when people discovered that it masked a vain, self-serving poseur whose principles came in and out with the Jones Beach tide. Benny's problem was not that he wanted to be all things to all people. It was, as he later explained succinctly in the title of his autobiography, a simple case of "All I Want Is Everything."

But Benny (who, by the way, had picked up his nickname for distributing Benzedrine as an undergraduate at Columbia) was the properly elected mayor and he had grown accustomed to bodyguards, limousines, and the deference of the people.

So his decision, as he put it, "to clean the streets of the city" with a massive police sweep of the homeless was in no way a matter of principle. It was a plainly political choice made in an increasingly frightened and reactionary city. It was designed to launch his fourth campaign for what he was convinced was "his" job.

It must be said, however, that Benny didn't do things halfway. The fact that there was no ideological consistency to his actions was muffled by the thunder of the events, in this case the mobilization of some fifteen thousand cops earning overtime. They formed a Roman phalanx on the grounds of the Dyckman public housing project on the northern edge of Manhattan and marched south, followed by a second line of paddy wagons that swept down each of the avenues. They scooped up anybody who looked shabby, tearing down cardboard shelters and seizing blankets and coffee cans filled with sad belongings. They dumped and set fire to a great mountain of steaming trash in the Central Park Sheep Meadow.

The homeless people themselves were jammed into the paddy wagons and trucked to Downing Stadium on Randalls Island where little campsites had been laid out inside a high wired enclosure.

Marigold was having a somewhat dusty fried egg sandwich for breakfast that morning when her first word of the sweep came from the Professor (Princeton, Ethics, you remember), who was on one of his periodic "sobers," as he called them, and thus was fully awake and functioning when the phone rang in the lobby of the Bond Hotel where he was still on retainer as a guard and doorman to Margaret "Pegleg" Malmsey.

The Professor, who wasn't very good at crisis management, panicked.

The front door of the Bond Hotel was just a block away from Marigold's grate, and the Professor flung himself through the door, jumped first on the hood and then the roof of Sam Ashby's brand-new blue car, and started screaming the kind of sentence you might expect from an overeducated alcoholic in high gear: "The British are coming! The British are coming!"

Mr. Ashby, manager of the Greek restaurant on the corner next to the hotel, came roaring out of his establishment. "Get off my car, you lunatic!" he screamed. But the Professor, holding a shaky balance on the roof, brought his forefinger to his lips and Sam Ashby stopped in his tracks and listened.

A few blocks uptown, a great sound was rumbling toward them. It was the sound of engines, great numbers of engines mixed with voices, whistles, and sirens. A great, eerie pandemonium was coming down the avenues.

The Professor looked helplessly into the eyes of Marigold, who had come to full alert.

"It's the big sweep, Marigold. God help us, it's the sweep."

At first, everyone was paralyzed by the sound, and then, suddenly, popping like a cork out of the bottleneck of Hubert Street, a stream of blue-shirted cops brandishing billy clubs and shouting obscenities formed a line that stretched from building to building all across West Broadway and advanced toward Marigold's grate and the folded figure of the Professor who was sitting atop Mr. Ashby's new blue Mercedes.

The blue line was still a full block away when two strange men in long gray dusters suddenly appeared from around the corner, swept the Professor off the top of the car with a single pass of a push broom, and then proceeded to cover Sam Ashby's Mercedes with a great red velveteen cloth.

It appears that the mayor had made special arrangements to see that the property of registered voters was protected from the powerful stream of adrenaline that poured out from the thin blue line of advancing policemen. In no time at all, dozens of little red hillocks appeared in the neighborhood as the gray-dustered guardians scurried through the community covering expensive cars and ten-speed bicycles.

Down the street came the police, sidestepping the bright red lumps and beating up the street people.

It had all happened so fast that Marigold had not even finished her egg sandwich or unwound herself from her blanket when four unearthly police officers wearing dark blue helmets and tinted plastic face guards picked her up by her four corners and passed her, high in the air, down a line of burly blue men to the open door of a paddy wagon where a white-smocked matron with a clipboard and a long, evil-looking ballpoint pen, assigned her a seat.

Thunder, whose pint of Wild Irish Rose had slipped from his pink waistband when he was lifted and passed over to another paddy wagon, was frantically wiggling his body and screaming, "My wine! My wine!" as he tore at his unraveling waistband.

The seventy-nine-cent bottle could have been found in the scoop end of a large coal shovel that had been shoved under all of Marigold and Thunder's worldly goods with a single thrust. The shovel was lifted in the air, rising like the host at the sacrifice of the Mass, and its contents dumped into the trash truck with some ceremony; one bottle, one blanket, four empty soda cans, three empty matchbook covers, one nickel, a polished brass doorknob, a Baggie full of rusty nails, a black plastic nameplate that said "Russia" in three languages, and two brand-new combs.

The Professor, who, as you will recall, had been swiped from the top of the blue Mercedes by a push broom, had miraculously broken none of his bones and had been able to stumble his way back into the lobby of the Bond Hotel where he sat down on the old rug and peered out below a pulled-down shade at the chaos in the streets.

On West Broadway, the Professor watched the rise and fall of the billy clubs and winced when he saw Pete, the proprietor of Savanah Liquors, cuffed and tossed into the paddy wagon. Pete objected to police carpenters who were covering the front of his store with plywood, carrying out another special order of the mayor who objected to the sale of any wine that had been dead for less than two years.

And Mayor Benny Brazil himself was sitting in his City Hall office a scant three blocks away, watching the sweep on an enormous live projection television screen. He had mixed emotions. He was gleeful as he watched a closeup of the plywood board nailed over Savannah Liquors. He toasted the scene with a crystal glassful of Château Mouton Rothschild '83, but he shuddered as the TV camera zoomed in on Thunder being clubbed into his seat in the departing paddy wagon. Thunder's image was four feet tall in the mayor's office. Thunder was finally on his knees, pleading to the camera, to the world, and literally to the mayor to return his precious half pint of Wild Irish Rose.

There was a knock on the mayor's door, and Grover, the mayor's chief of protocol, stepped into the room, grasped the bottle of champagne, and sputtered, "My God, Benny, the eighty-three Mouton! I thought we were saving it for the election."

"What election?" shouted the mayor. "Look at that face, Grover! Look at that goddamn pathetic vote-killer face!" The mayor ran over to the TV screen and stuck his thumb on Thunder's nose, which was getting smaller and smaller as the paddy wagon headed east toward Randalls Island.

The mayor turned savagely to Grover. "This was your idea, Grover. 'Clean 'em up,' you said. 'Make 'em disappear,' you said. *They can't vote!* you said. Well, goddamn it, this thing is on *six channels,* and the ratings will go through the roof. And do you know who owns television sets, Grover? Do you know?"

The mayor was shaking his chief of protocol by the scruff of his neck. "Voters! That's who, Grover. *My* voters!"

Grover looked down at his hand, which was still holding the priceless champagne. "What the hell," he said and took a swig, straight from the bottle.

AT THAT VERY moment, the Professor stepped fearfully out of the front door of the Bond Hotel and looked over the battlefield. It was mostly silent, except for the plaint of a couple of cats. You could even hear the Tribeca wind as it tossed aluminum cans against the concrete curb. And West Broadway seemed to have the measles: little bright red bumps of covered cars had broken out everywhere. But to the Professor, the empty street seemed wasted and sad until an odd flash of pink caught his eye over near the liquor store where the paddy wagon had been loaded. He gingerly walked across the street, being careful not to disturb the cover on Sam Ashby's Mercedes. There on the sidewalk, spread out in all its tiny glory, was Thunder's pink waistband. For the first time since he had been fired from Princeton, the Professor cried.

THUNDER WAS PISSED, *very* pissed. Not only had he lost his wine and his waistband, but he couldn't find Marigold in what was fast becoming the great campground of Downing Stadium. Street people had been pouring in all day, and by the time the West Broadway paddy wagons arrived, at least a thousand citizens covered with khaki blankets had staked out their campsites inside the high wire fence that ran around the playing field. As the sun went down, small clusters of poor people, hooded against the cold October evening air, sat around small sputtering fires made mostly from the paper plates that the Salvation Army had set out next to five steaming oilcans full of excellent chili.

Many were hurt, and since no doctors, nurses, or ambulances had been brought in to help them, the people around the campfires tended to one another, bringing them closer together as evening came.

The first person Thunder met as he wandered from fire to fire searching for Marigold was Flash Gordon who had slipped under the wire fence. He stuck out like a sore thumb with his black fedora and clean white shirt.

Flash was jubilant. "Thunder!" he cried, wrapping Thunder in his arms. "This is it! Benny Brazil has finally screwed up. We'll take him in a walk!"

Flash turned to the campground spread out before him and softly spoke to the nearest couple of campfires.

"Marigold for mayor," he said softly, confidentially.

"By the way," he added quietly to Thunder, "where the hell is Marigold?"

"Right here," answered Marigold, who was standing four feet away holding out an uncapped pint bottle of wine to Thunder.

At that moment, Thunder, who couldn't remember a moment in his life when he had not been sitting, standing, or sleeping next to Marigold, collapsed into her arms, and the two of them went tumbling to the ground, kicking and kissing, laughing and smacking but holding the open bottle of Wild Irish Rose in a vertical position.

Their frolic done, they rather sheepishly took their usual position, sitting on the ground with Thunder's head on Marigold's shoulder.

Marigold spoke with considerable poise. "A bad thing was done today, old Flash. My friends have been hurt because they live outdoors. And I nearly lost my Thunder on this October afternoon. I don't know what I'm going to do because I'm very tired and need to sleep. In the morning, I'll decide."

And with the grace of a great fairy queen, Marigold kicked aside some orange peels and chili plates. With her prince in her arms, she went to sleep.

Flash was content. He looked around him and saw the tiny fires of Agincourt, the campfires of the queen's army as they were extinguished one by one.

In City Hall, Benny Brazil prowled the basement corridor, slamming his fist in his hand each time he heard a gust of laughter coming from the cocktail party two floors above, spilling out of the Board of Estimate chambers and onto the great marble steps that led to the lobby. The party had been planned as a postsweep celebration for all his most generous friends.

"Those goddamn idiots, don't they know what we've done? We've handed the city to Bleeder Bender! Bleeder Goddamn Bender!"

A short explanation of the electoral civics of New York City might be helpful here. Benny Brazil had been the mayor for eleven years. As mentioned above, he won his first election handily, affecting a saucy but bogus free spirit. Benny was a Democrat. His perennial Republican-Liberal opponent was Arnold "Bleeder" Bender, a starry-eyed lightweight who was, it seems, always on the edge of tears, pining for his fellow man. Benny had, at first, made short work of the Bleeder, but each succeeding election had been closer as Benny's true nature as a finger-wagging reactionary revealed itself. This year, Benny had actually almost lost the primary to a resourceful and sunny rascal named George Faucet who was defeated on election eve by a photograph on the front of the *New York Post* showing him cockeyed drunk and naked with a saucepan on his head at a preelection party in the Goldfish Room at the Summit Hotel. The absolute truth is that George Faucet had been suckered into the Goldfish Room by Grover, Benny's chief of protocol.

But that was old news. Benny's latest problem with the homeless sweep was compounded by the fact that the Bleeder had hired the big-time, internationally celebrated PR firm of Polonaise Inc. to dry Bleeder's tears and generally recast his image into a take-charge, clean-as-a-whistle re-former.

The sweep had, in fact, been Grover's idea. Grover considered himself a master political tactician and had been right so many times in the past eleven years that Benny had approved the sweep, which, as Grover knew, catered to Benny's worst instinct, a contempt for the homeless that made him a fan of the caste system of untouchables that had flourished in colonial India.

So, as Benny paced the basement corridors of City Hall that evening, he knew the following: One, the homeless sweep had been a terrible blunder. In Thunder's pleading face he could see hundreds of thousands of votes go aglimmering. Two, Polonaise Inc. had obviously arranged for the comprehensive all-channel coverage of the sweep, and that meant that Arnold "Bleeder" Bender had decided to stop losing. And three, Benny was going to be goddamned if he was gonna lose this election.

Almost mystically, a complicated plan formed in his mind.

Two floors above the mayor, Grover was drunk. After eleven years of faithful service, the mayor had insulted him, actually laid hands upon him, doubted his judgment, and demoralized him to the point that he had chugalugged Château Mouton Rothschild. So he was not at his best when the cocktail buzz on the marble steps suddenly stopped and the mayor popped out of the elevator and into the party with his best political smile in place.

"Grover!" the mayor called, out walking by a nest of admirers and putting his mouth next to Grover's ear. "We're gonna play it *both* ways," he whispered.

Benny Brazil then turned to his assembled supporters. "I propose a toast!" he announced, lifting another skinny glass, "to the New York City Police Department! To the brave men and women who civilized our streets today!"

"But you said—" blurted Grover.

"I said thank you!" hollered the mayor. "Thank you, Grover! Ladies and gentlemen," he lifted his glass again, "I give you Grover! The man who swept the homeless from the streets!"

"I did?" said Grover and he shook a hundred hands.

Wednesday, October 25, Day Two

The dawn was October red at the great campground on Randalls Island as the campsites began to stir. Normally, Marigold and Thunder were wide awake by rush hour in order to panhandle the hurrying people, but during the night they had been awakened four or five times by a stream of well-meaning Upper East Side delegations dispensing bandages and blankets, cots, air mattresses, Coleman stoves, and all manner of food.

Everything, indeed, except money.

At about ten A.M., Flash came over to Marigold's encampment with three steaming cups of black coffee in his hand and was invited to sit down.

"Well," said Flash, "have you heard? The mayor's coming. He's gonna make a speech."

209

"We will be silent," said Marigold immediately.

"Silent?" asked Flash.

"Silent as the potter's field," she said.

The events of the past day had placed a harp string in Marigold's tongue.

"Not a word. Not a sound," she added.

Thunder was already on his feet, running from campfire to campfire spreading the word. "No one is supposed to talk when the mayor get's here! It's Marigold's idea. No one speaks! Not a word. Not a sound. Watch Marigold!"

LESS THAN AN hour later, wonderful things began to happen all over the campground.

Back in Manhattan, the Professor had summoned up a small miracle. First, he scoured the East Village for all of its magicians, jugglers, and clowns. And, as he had done two Christmases ago, he organized them into a small parade led by Marigold's own Salvation Army band. Trooping along as usual, playing the wrong music to march by, the band and its motley following crossed the footbridge at East 103rd Street and arrived at the stadium. They were immediately admitted by brown-uniformed traffic cops who had, in the middle of the night, on instructions of the mayor, replaced the original ring of armed and helmeted riot police.

Over on the south end of the playing field, four jugglers flung tenpins at each other, a magician made Marigold's pal Agnes disappear in a puff of smoke, and two high-wire walkers danced along the horizontal bars of the football goals at each end of the field.

The Salvation Army band was soon outclassed by a pickup band of New York Philharmonic wannabees who decided to play the entire canon of John Philip Sousa, giving the already exciting scene a foot-stomping, martial air.

In truth, the homeless folks, who had been dragged kicking and screaming into the paddy wagons only the day before, hardly knew what to make of it all and huddled closer to their campfires or migrated to the north end of the field where Pete from Savannah Liquors, who had managed a round-trip for supplies from Tribeca, had set up shop inside four football sideline benches arranged in a square.

IT WAS THUNDER who first heard the siren-screaming, light-flashing parade of blue and white police cars roar down the off-ramp from the Triborough Bridge and onto the island. Behind the first four cars was the mayor's famous Tactical Bus, which, over the years, had become a little sillier each time it was used, as the mayor chased felonies and fires dressed up in an orange vest, carrying two walkie-talkies and a pearl-handled revolver. This time, the bus came to a loud stop at the front gate of the stadium, and Grover jumped out with a portable lectern followed by two assistants carrying a bulky digital sound system. At first there was much excitement as Grover and his men stepped very politely around small campsites in order to set up the lectern and the sound system dead center in the middle of the playing field.

Then the press bus and trucks emptied out, disgorging reporters, transmission dishes, cables, and fuzzy-faced white gaffers who wore sunglasses and carried small Evian bottles in their fanny packs.

Back in the mayor's Tactical Bus, Benny Brazil was trying to decide what to wear. The orange reflecting vest and the revolver seemed a bit much, and he had just worn the Hard Rock Café T-shirt to a ceremony at the Waldorf. His only choice was his trademark red suspenders over a striped shirt and chino jeans.

The mayor's walkie-talkie squawked, "This is Sycophant. This is Sycophant. Over."

Benny pressed the talk button. "Five by five, Sycophant. This is Master Builder. Are we ready, Grover?"

"Do I have to be 'Sycophant,' Benny?" crackled Grover.

"If you like your job, Sycophant," said Master Builder.

"That's a roger, Master Builder," said Sycophant.

"I'm going with the red suspenders and the chinos. What do you think?"

"I think that's fine. Everybody seems friendly, Master Builder."

Indeed, since Grover and his assistants had arrived on the field, they had been mobbed by happy jugglers and clowns. Even several of the hooded homeless people who had been plucked out of Penn Station the day before gathered around the lectern as Grover solemnly placed the great seal of the City of New York on the front of the lectern below a cluster of microphones.

"Here I come," squawked Master Builder as he braced himself, handed his walkie-talkie to the bus driver, and stood bravely on the rubber steps of the bus as the double doorway opened with a gentle *woosh.*

There, directly in front of him, their arms locked together, stood Marigold and Thunder.

The mayor immediately recognized Thunder's face from the TV screen in his office and involuntarily recoiled, backing up a full step into the bus.

Marigold was holding her finger to her lips.

Slowly, all over the stadium, voices began to stop. The fuzzy gaffers, chattering as they uncoiled their cables, stopped and turned toward the tableau at the front gate. The high-wire walkers jumped down from the goal posts and the clowns became mimes. The sound was pinched off at each of the campsites as everyone turned to watch Marigold stand before the mayor. Grover was still barking orders to his assistants until he realized that his voice was the only voice echoing in the stadium. Embarrassed, he stopped and turned, facing the gate with the others.

A great silence descended on the island. Only the odd *cawk* of swooping seagulls and the very very distant low rattle of the city could be heard. Each time a mystified drunk squealed "Wha's happening, where'd everybody go?" he was immediately squelched by his companions. The interruptions made the silence grow deeper and more profound.

"Good morning!" quacked the mayor, and he held out his hand to Marigold.

With sovereign elegance Marigold bowed slightly from the waist and then turned her back.

As did the entire gathering.

Everyone, from the miming clowns to the khaki homeless, turned their backs on the mayor. As if by a magic spell, the people turned their backs.

The mayor stood there for a full minute, options racing through his mind. He glanced over at the lectern and saw that even Grover had been captured by the silence and stood staring up at the seagulls diving toward Manhattan, his back to Master Builder.

Benny grabbed his walkie-talkie and whispered, "Sycophant. Come in, Sycophant. This is Master Builder."

But Grover had accidentally leaned his walky-talky against the microphone on the lectern, so the mayor's hushed voice could be heard in every corner of the stadium.

"Sycophant. Come in, Sycophant," echoed through the campground. "This is Master Builder. Let's get the hell out of here. You were right, these bums can't vote."

At first, a great common shock went through the stadium, and then everyone began to laugh, and great rainsheets of laughter swept through the multitude. Even Marigold and Thunder were clapping each other on the back as they laughed. The reporters and the gaffers laughed, the clowns and wire walkers and the homeless people laughed. Even the cops laughed until the stadium rocked with merriment and the jugglers started tossing their tenpins again, and the band struck up "Stars and Stripes Forever" for the fourth time as Pete from Savannah Liquors ripped open a new case of Thunderbird.

In the midst of all this laughter, the mayor retreated into the Tactical Bus, and the driver, trying hard to contain himself, started the engine. The half dozen police cruisers came to life, started by giggling officers. Then an unsmiling Grover raced for the bus, squeezing between the closing doors just in time. He had left the lectern and its sound system behind.

As the caravan of buses, trucks, and police cars roared back up the on-ramp onto the Triborough Bridge, the last thing the mayor heard on Randalls Island was a rousing cheer that bloomed from the campground as Marigold stepped toward the lectern in the center of the field.

Flash knocked on the microphone to make sure it was working and then gallantly gave Marigold his hand and she stepped up onto the platform to stand before her people.

"Can you hear me?" called out Marigold.

"Just fine," answered Thunder, and then the crowd repeated, "Fine!"

"My friend Flash has asked me to run for mayor, and I guess I'm gonna do it."

A cheer exploded.

"Now wait a minute! Wait a minute!" But the crowd would not be silenced and the roar got louder and louder. Marigold was trying to speak. She said, "I won't play the fool . . . ," but by that time she had been lifted to the shoulders of her nearest khaki-shrouded friends and passed along the top of the crowd. The Salvation Army band struck up "Nearer My God to Thee" and other unmarchable tunes, and Randalls Island rang with joy.

When the mayor and his entourage left, they left the gate open. In a few hours, when Pete's last pint was drained, everybody went home.

Thursday, October 26, Day Three

When Arnold "Bleeder" Bender, Republican candidate for mayor, woke up the next morning, Sam Silk, president of Bleeder's PR firm, tossed a copy of the *Daily News* onto Bleeder's enormous belly.

In three-inch-high letters, the headline yelled: "THESE BUMS CAN'T VOTE!"

And just below it, slightly smaller: "MAYOR LOSES IT AT HOMELESS RALLY."

And just below *that*, even smaller: "Homeless Woman Says She'll Run for Mayor."

Bleeder knew most of the details of Benny Brazil's faux pas with the amplifier, having been briefed by a wildly enthusiastic team from Polonaise Inc. the night before. But he searched the article that followed for some word about this mysterious "homeless woman" who had showed up. The article said, in part:

> Byron Lord Gordon, known as "Flash," a well-known local public relations expert, announced that Marigold, an African-American homeless woman, was joining the race for mayor today.

216

"Since the primaries are over," said Gordon to this re-
porter, "Marigold will run as a write-in candidate, but a
write-in candidate with a difference—she fully intends to
win.

"The savage behavior of Mayor Benny Brazil in order-
ing a sweep of the homeless and their detention on Randalls Island two days ago, plus his open contempt for the
poor in a visit to the island yesterday, smacks of the geno-
cidal thuggery in Europe earlier in this century."

"I want that guy Gordon on *my* team," said Arnold
"Bleeder" Bender as he floundered out of bed.

"He is! He is!" said Sam Silk. "This Marigold is made
in heaven for us. The bigger she gets, the harder Benny
falls."

"But what if she wins?" said Bleeder. "I like her!"

"She won't, Bleeder, and do you wanta know why?"

"Why?"

"Because these bums *can't* vote. They don't live anyplace, and to vote in this country you've got to live someplace. You gotta have a 'domicile.' "

Bleeder had his third croissant.

When Sam Silk made that pronouncement to Bleeder
Bender, he didn't know that Flash Gordon, from the moment he heard the mayor utter the words "These bums
can't vote," had gotten up his constitutional dander. Calling together a meeting of aging civil rights lawyers on
Thursday afternoon, Flash and his old pals from the sixties filed suit in the New York State Supreme Court

(*Marigold et al.* v. *The New York City Board of Elections*) demanding that the Baxter Street Shelter and one hundred and sixty other shelters throughout the city, large and small, be declared official "domiciles" for those who passed through their doors.

Sitting on the case was Judge Laura "Bunny" Lake, Flash's ex-wife from thirty years ago who had left Flash when he was trying to drown in a puddle of booze. He and Bunny had remained friends as Judge Lake's career had blossomed. Flash laid low during the hearing so that Bunny wouldn't recuse herself.

Friday, October 27, Day Four

West Broadway, from Vesey Street all the way up to Hubert, had been transformed. Most of the red measles bumps had been left in place by sympathetic car owners; indeed, Sam Ashby couldn't believe his luck as print and electronic reporters poured into his restaurant which, as you remember, was next to the Bond Hotel.

Now, by the grace of God, the Bond Hotel (owner Peggy "Pegleg" Malmsey had turned into a religious zealot) had become Marigold for Mayor headquarters.

God, by the way, had instructed Peggy to donate twenty-nine hundred dollars to the Marigold campaign, which meant that the lobby was soon filled up with telephones and blackboards.

Flash called everybody, especially his media pals at Hurley's bar, who came en masse to see that the Marigold candidacy was properly covered. Everybody tried Pete's

Wild Irish Rose. Much to Thunder's amusement, they disguised their horror out of respect for Marigold. Although a perfectly fine, warm room off the lobby of the Bond Hotel had been set aside for Marigold and Thunder, they stubbornly insisted on staying on their grate, Marigold supervising the installation of literally hundreds of banners and crepe-paper streamers all up and down the street. Marigold was overheard to say, "We're having guests. We've got to gussy up this slum."

The Professor, who was drinking again and therefore available only half of each day, fell naturally into the role of actor-manager, placing the Salvation Army band on the triangular island between Chambers and Reade streets and scattering the jugglers and magicians throughout the neighborhood to recapture the splendid joy of the final night at Randalls Island.

Flash and his now-gigantic staff of students, aging Freedom Riders, and street urchins tended to the serious business of the campaign. Curious power brokers made their way to the Bond Hotel and Marigold's grate. Even "Bleeder," against the advice of his Polonaise Inc. advisers, made a brief pilgrimage to West Broadway and, to everyone's surprise, left very quickly after a short and confidential chat with Marigold. He was smiling.

One final touch. Thomas Borowik, an old friend of Flash's and owner of the Tisket-Tasket Novelty Company, had two hundred thousand bright yellow paper marigolds with peel-off backings printed and distributed virtually overnight. They bloomed all over the city.

Monday, October 30, Day Seven

At two in the afternoon, the State Supreme Court issued an interim order, which in effect permitted anyone who had resided in any of the formal city homeless shelters and "were otherwise eligible to vote" to register and vote in the fast-approaching mayoral election. The order was signed by Judge Laura Lake.

Now understand, Judge Lake's order affected fewer than ten thousand potential voters, hardly enough to alter a traditional New York City mayoral election. And since Marigold was running a write-in campaign, there was serious doubt as to whether the newly franchised voters could manage the mechanics of standing upright in a booth and writing "Marigold" in the proper place. In this regard, Marigold's best buddy Agnes immediately organized handwriting practice groups using five cargo pallets from Bazzini's as a simulated voting booth.

Tuesday, October 31, Day Eight

In the morning the New York *Daily News* straw poll changed everything. Apparently, the live broadcast of Benny Brazil's homeless sweep, his subsequent humiliation on Randalls Island, and two hundred thousand marigolds stuck on everybody's lapel had cut deeply into the mayor's eleven-year core of voters. The poll showed Arnie "Bleeder" Bender at 27 percent, Benny Brazil at 14 percent, and Marigold leading at 39 percent, with a solid 20 percent undecided. The straw poll exclusively questioned registered voters, so Marigold's brand-new bunch of voters were suddenly serious players who could put her over the top.

Benny Brazil, alone in his City Hall basement office, muttered, "No more Mister Nice Guy."

Wednesday, November I, Day Nine
Four top executives of Polonaise Inc. were seen entering City Hall though the back entrance opposite the Tweed Courthouse at midnight on Wednesday evening.

Monday, November 6, Day Fourteen
The scandal broke in Monday morning's *New York Post*. Beautifully timed, it actually screamed:

HOMELESS PHONY!
ELECTION FRAUD!
MARIGOLD IS AN HEIRESS!

The story was by-lined Richard Finley-Farragut, a convicted sleazeball masquerading as an investigative journalist. Finley-Farragut had received a three A.M. phone call Thursday morning advising him to check out one Sarah Sweet, now deceased, who had lived and died in Harlem on top of a stash of negotiable Housing Authority bonds. The bonds were worth eleven million dollars at present rates, and the sole heir to this fortune was one Marigold Sweet, Sarah's actress daughter who had spent the past eighteen months posing as an indigent homeless woman in preparation for her role in a cinema verité film to be entitled *Scavenger*.

Marigold, according to Finley-Farragut, returned each evening at two A.M. to Harlem to take a bath.

Flash was hysterical. The story was a total fiction. There was no Sarah Sweet, no money, and no movie. But it *was* Monday, the day before the election, and with no afternoon newspapers, it was impossible to fight back in print.

"In print," he repeated to himself.

Flash called a massive electronic press conference.

When she read the *Post* that morning, Marigold had suddenly become pensive. Even Thunder couldn't understand. "Flash'll fix this up," said Thunder, slamming the tabloid in the nearest waste can. "Everything's gonna be all right, you'll see."

"It will indeed," said Marigold.

Marigold had waved off a briefing by Flash before the press conference and spent two and a half hours in the beauty parlor refurbishing her famous towering hairdo. The enormous gathering of press broke out in spontaneous applause when she emerged from the hairdresser in all her glory, her hair a great trophy on the top of her head, and wearing another pink paper duster that in the glare of the TV lights looked once again like a royal crimson robe.

Everyone was there: live TV cameras from every station, radio reporters, a Japanese videotape crew, Swedes, Germans, and Italians. *The Irish Echo* sent a man, and there in the front sat Richard Finley-Farragut, author of the morning screed.

Thunder dusted off the old aluminum kitchen chair that had a yellow seat, and Marigold sat down.

"First of all," she said, "I want to tell you, Mr. Farragut, that you have made a terrible mistake. I'm sure you'll set it right once I tell you that I have no mother that I know of, never had.

"I am what I appear to be, what Flash would call a vagabond, a tramp who's perched upon your shoulder. I am no more than that," she stopped and raised her hand slightly from her knee for emphasis, "nor am I less.

"I am not a proper candidate for mayor—I drink too much.

"The mayor is not a proper candidate for mayor—he hates too much.

"I got my hair done, as you see." She pointed to the beauticians lined up behind her. "Ladies, take a bow."

She looked directly into the camera. "From time to time we need reminding that the world is filled with people unfulfilled. I lost my head and ran for mayor because I thought the mayor had lost his mind.

"I love the marigolds you wear and hope that everyone who wore a marigold or planned to vote for me tomorrow will vote for Mr. Bender who is, I think, a fat but gentle man."

At that moment, a kettledrum of thunder cracked across the Hudson River sky. An ocean of rain fell on West Broadway, scattering reporters, bums, and jugglers far and wide. Within minutes, the great banners and paper marigolds, the red velveteen covers and the crepe-paper streamers, were washed from the street into a river of a dozen colors that flowed into the sewers.

Tuesday, November 7, Election Day

"Bleeder" Bender won, going away.

For a moment there, it seemed as if something extraordinary had happened in the city. But now it was over, swept away.

For Marigold and for her friends, nothing had changed.

426f0